GOD OF WAR

NICHOLE ROSE, NICHOLE FALLON

Cover by Angela Haddon Designs

Paperback Cover by Artscandare Designs

CONTENTS

ABOUT THE BOOK

There are no rules in love and war. There's only pillage and conquer. And this wicked prince could teach lessons in both.

You take from me, and I destroy the thing you love most. Everyone knows that's how I operate. So when the head of the Irish mob puts his filthy hands in my business, it shouldn't come as a surprise when I put mine on his pretty little daughter.

I expected a jaded Irish princess, not an innocent little lamb. But there's something about Brynna Sullivan that's magnetic, drawing me to her light. I don't want to destroy it. I want to claim it as my own...wreck her, and then put her back together again.

But this fiery little princess isn't naïve. She knows exactly who and what I am. And convincing her to fall for a monster like me Well, it'll take all-out war.

But this is one battle I intend to win, no matter what it takes. I just didn't expect it to be my own people who betrayed me in the end...

God of War is a dark mafia romance featuring an unapologetic villain, a strong, curvy heroine, and all the spice. Can Naz and Brynna overcome the odds stacked against them and find forever together, or will their fierce connection crumble under the weight of their reality?

CONTENT ADVISORY

This is a dark romance full of dark delights.

If you're looking for a good guy hero, you won't find him here. But if you want a villain who knows he's a villain, one who will burn the world for the one he loves, takes no prisoners, and makes no apologies, meet Naz.

Please check the TWs on my website here.

Reader discretion is advised.

CHAPTER ONE

Naz

"What is this?" I ask, flicking my gaze up from the report Nicolas Arias just placed on the desk in front of me.

"The report you requested, *príncipe*."

I draw a deep breath, a muscle in my jaw ticking with impatience. "The last time I checked, I was buying this company. So why is Nolan Sullivan now listed as the owner of record?"

"Ah, he is playing dirty games again." Nicolas sneers, his full lips twisting as he relays the news. "He bought the company out from under you."

Jesus Christ. That's the third time this year that Nolan Sullivan has messed with my shit. As soon as I set my sights on a company, he sweeps in and snaps it up. It's beginning to piss me off.

I don't fuck with the Irish mob and their businesses. I'm not sure why Sullivan has made it his mission to fuck with me and mine.

"And how did he find out I put in an offer on Roheim International, Nicolas?" I growl, drumming my fingers against the calendar on my desk. That's the important question as far as I'm concerned.

Being cut out once is random. Twice could be a coincidence. But three times in a year? That's intentional. It's a fucking declaration of war.

Nicolas hesitates for a long moment, rubbing his thumb along his bottom lip like he always does when he's about to deliver news he knows I won't like. The man is nothing if not predictable. "I believe he has people on the inside, Naz."

"A fucking rat," I say, wanting it spoken plainly. No need to beat around the bush. Nolan Sullivan is fucking with my money. And someone on my payroll is feeding the motherfucker the information to do it.

"I believe so." Nicolas grimaces, his heavy brows furrowed over sharp hazel eyes. "It isn't like when your father was *barón*, *príncipe*. Loyalty is everything, but some of these Americans have no concept of the word, no? They blow where the wind takes them."

I eye him levelly, my patience dwindling in the face of his familiar complaint. I've heard it a dozen times in the last two months alone.

Nicolas Arias dreams of the glory days when my father led our family. Unfortunately for him, the glory days died when my father, his wife, and my half-siblings were murdered by Felipe Rojas and his men, leaving me the only remaining heir to the Leyva empire.

To save me from the same fate, my mother—my father's American mistress—insisted I be raised in the country that birthed me. Nicolas has been stuck here since I was a teenager, dreaming of home. I was born here. I've lived here exclusively since I was eleven. I lead from my goddamn throne here—safely out of reach of Rojas and his cartel. Nicolas conveniently forgets all of that when lodging his complaints, however.

He's the only one who would dare—my oldest friend, my closest advisor. He's both the angel and devil on my shoulders.

"And I suppose the wind took them and my business dealings to Sullivan?" I ask, eyeing him levelly.

"It appears so." His lips twitch with amusement. He's trying to be funny, but I'm not laughing.

I crumple up the report, tossing it in the trashcan beside my desk. "Find out who the fuck is leaking my information, Nicolas," I growl. "I want them dealt with now."

He hesitates, opening and closing his mouth like he has something to say.

"That wasn't a suggestion," I snap, not in the mood for whatever other bullshit he's going to toss my way. I needed that fucking company to help facilitate product shipments into international ports. With recent crackdowns, moving our product out of Colombia has gotten more complicated. The more ships we have moving legitimate products, the easier it is to hide the things we need hidden—like the drugs and money.

The last thing I need is Nolan Sullivan in my business, throwing a wrench into the works. The man isn't even in the cocaine business. He owns a goddamn high-end nightclub he uses to distribute the ecstasy his people funnel through the city. The prick only wants my ships so I can't have them.

"I'll look into it, Naz," Nicolas promises. "But you've ignored his meddling so far. Perhaps it's time for a more direct approach, no? Remind him who he messes with."

"Are you telling me how to run things?" I ask, my voice cold. He may be my oldest friend, but no one tells me what the fuck to do. Not even him.

"No." He holds up his hands in a placating gesture. "Of course not, Naz. I merely mean...our people call you *Dios de la Guerra,* the god of war, for a reason." A sly smile flashes across his face. "Perhaps it is time for Sullivan to learn exactly what that means, no?"

The god of war. *Cristo.* I'm fairly certain Nicolas is the one who gave me that particular name. I'm not sure what infuriates me more. The fact that it stuck...or the fact that it isn't far from the truth.

I haven't known peace since...actually, I don't think I've ever known peace. I was born in war. Rojas and my father were battling it out before I was even born. And I've been at war with that prick ever since. He isn't the only one. I have more enemies than I can count. And I've killed more than I remember.

Peace? It's a pipe dream not meant for motherfuckers like me.

"You can go now," I mutter wearily. "Find out exactly who the fuck is spying for Sullivan, Nicolas. I want the prick on his knees in front of me."

"Of course, *príncipe.*" Nicolas dips his head. "I meant no disrespect."

I don't respond. He never means any disrespect, but he skirts the line anyway. He's old school, old guard. And he still remembers when I was a teenager, trying to wear this crown and bury my mother at the same damn time. It wasn't pretty. Nothing I do ever is.

He's right, though. It is time for a more direct approach. It's been time for a while.

I wait for my office door to click closed behind him before pulling open my desk drawer and reaching inside.

I grab the photo on top, lifting it out. My gaze runs over the image.

"Brynna Sullivan," I murmur, eyes locked on the girl staring up at me. She's gorgeous in a way that's unsettling. Long red hair frames an angelic, heart-shaped face. Her skin is so translucent I can trace the veins beneath. Ample curves have my hands itching to know what they feel like beneath my fingers.

It's those fucking eyes that really get me, though. They're the clearest green I've ever seen, staring right out of the image and into my fucking soul.

In the photo, she's fresh-faced. Innocent. There's a fascinating purity to her, like the harshness of our world hasn't touched her. It's bullshit, though. In this world, no one is truly innocent. We've all got blood on our hands. We're all guilty.

Her father certainly is. His list of crimes is as long as my own.

And if he wants to fuck with my business, there's a price to pay. His family. Specifically, his pretty little daughter.

The only thing in this world he gives a shit about are his kids. It's a well-known fact that he dotes on her and her older brother, Niall. They want for nothing, lack nothing, and are threatened by nothing.

Until now.

If he wants war, so be it. I'll fight...but I'm not fighting fair. He took something that belonged to me. I'm taking something that belongs to him.

Who knows? I may even let him have her back when I'm done.

I stroke my thumb down the photo, my cock throbbing in anticipation.

Or maybe I won't.

CHAPTER TWO

Brynna

I close my eyes and inhale deeply as my fingers dance over cracked leather spines. The smell of old ink and musty, yellowed paper hovers in the air around me, bringing an instant smile to my face.

I could live in here and not regret a single second of it.

"Brynna, are you even listening to me?" My older brother, Niall, clearly isn't on the same page as me. His disgruntled question rips me right out of my happy bubble, plunking me down in cold, hard reality.

I prefer the happy bubble.

"Nope," I say cheerfully, just to rile him up. "Didn't hear a word."

In actuality, I heard everything he said. I was just trying to pretend the nonsense he's spouting about a charity gala is someone else's reality instead of my own. I'd much prefer to stay right here all day, thank you very much.

"Dammit," he growls. "Can you please be serious? This is important."

"So is this. Bookstore. Literature presentation. Half of my grade...ringing any bells?" I ask, only partially teasing. If he had his way, I wouldn't be in college right now. I'd be at home with him and our father, safely tucked away behind our mountainous walls, and whichever of their men drew the babysitting-Brynna-for-the-day straw.

Never mind the fact that I'm twenty-one years old and more than capable of babysitting myself. In their world—our world—I'm to be protected at all costs. It's more than mildly infuriating. It's also precisely why I started college two years later than everyone else.

It took me that freaking long to convince them to let me go. Campus is my sanctuary, the one place in the world where I'm actually free of the pressures of being...well, me. I'm not Brynna Sullivan, daughter of Nolan Sullivan, Irish mobster, when I'm at school. I'm just Brynna, boring college student.

At least, I would be if they'd leave me alone for longer than five minutes at a time. As soon as class ends for the day, my phone is ringing. It's exhausting, honestly.

Who does a girl have to kill to get a little peace and quiet?

Everyone, apparently.

"Shit," my brother mutters. "Forgot about that. How long are you going to be?"

"Depends on how long you intend to keep me on the phone." I pluck a copy of *War and Peace* from the shelf, rifling through it. It's ancient, the pages so well worn the ink has faded in places. "If you'd leave me alone, I could pick a book already."

"Fine, fine," he says. "But hurry, will you? 'Da says you still need to do a final fitting for your dress."

"Crap. The dress."

"Forgot, didn't you?"

"I didn't forget. I momentarily misremembered."

Niall laughs. "You are so full of shit."

"I get it honest."

"Yeah, you do." Another deep chuckle rolls down the line. "Just hurry it up, will you? And enjoy your dusty, boring bullshit."

"Only people who don't read call books dusty, boring bullshit, Niall." I roll my eyes, beyond being offended. He puts up a good front, but we both know his mind is a fascinating place. If he weren't tethered to the family business, the man could be anything. But Niall is...complicated.

I think he actually enjoys being Second-in-Command to our father. He enjoys breaking the law. He enjoys hiding it. He enjoys getting away with it. The man just enjoys doing all the wrong things. He gets it honest. Our father is the same way.

Dad could be a legitimate businessman. He simply chooses not to do it. He likes being the head of a criminal enterprise. Power is enthralling to him. The cold viciousness of their lifestyle feeds something in his soul. It's the same way for Niall. They thrive on chaos.

It scares me to think that there may be some part of me that's the same way. I don't want to be attracted to the life they lead. I don't want any part of my soul to identify with it. Yet sometimes, I think it might.

Why else do I accept that they are who they are? Why else is it so easy for me to pretend this world isn't as fucked up as it is? I'm complicit in their crimes, and I say nothing. Do nothing. I just...accept it.

I hide from the truth in books because the truth scares me. Books are safer. They're kinder. They understand the parts of my soul that ache for something different. For the freedom to admit who and what I really am.

In books, I can be all the messed-up parts of myself, and they don't judge me for it.

I appreciate that because I judge myself enough.

"See you soon," Niall says before hanging up on me.

"See you soon," I sigh, shoving my phone into my pocket. For a minute, I just stand there, staring into space. I'd much rather skip the damn charity gala altogether than spend yet another night pretending the money my father gives to charity makes up for all the terrible things he and my brother do to make said money. If there's a drug epidemic in this city, they had their hands in creating it. Spilling money into the coffers of the groups trying to clean it up is so damn sadly ironic it's painful. It shouldn't be that way.

But if wishes were wings...well, Niall wouldn't be blowing up my phone constantly, that's for sure. I'd actually have a little real independence instead of the illusion of it I've carved out for myself. My family would be at peace instead of constantly at war with some new enemy, and I wouldn't constantly have to look over my shoulder, wondering when the next attack is going to come.

And in this world, there's always a next attack.

I flick my gaze down at the book in my hand.

"War and Peace," I murmur, tucking the book under my arm. I'm doing my presentation on it. Why not? For a book as old as this one, Tolstoy's themes are a little too relevant to my life.

I spend a few more minutes browsing, picking up several more books to add to my collection, before I turn and head for the front counter. That ridiculous dress isn't going to fit itself. Unfortunately.

I turn the corner, worried about the dress for tomorrow's gala, when I collide with what feels like a solid wall.

"Shit," a man growls, grasping for me.

My books fall from my hands, scattering across the floor as I stumble back, nearly losing my balance.

"I'm so sorry!" Cheeks burning, I drop to my knees to gather the mess of books now scattered across the dusty floor at my feet.

The man kneels to help in his expensive suit. My gaze travels up his muscular arms to broad shoulders and a chiseled jaw. His face is a study in sharp angles and smooth planes, his cheekbones high and defined. Intense amber eyes pin me in place as they lock with mine.

Recognition slams into me like a freight train, turning my blood to ice.

Nazario Leyva. My father's nemesis. He's also one of the most dangerous men in this city.

Why is he here?

Do I even need to ask? I've had a target painted on my back since the day I was born. This wouldn't be the first time one of my father's enemies tried to get to him through me. It happens so fucking often it's honestly exhausting. But this one stings. Campus is supposed to be my safe haven, the one place in this city where my father's world doesn't intrude.

If Nazario is here, his world hasn't just intruded. It's packed up and moved in.

Lovely.

"Let me help you with that, *cariño*," Nazario murmurs, his voice a low rumble that vibrates through me. He moves with a fascinating predatory grace as he quickly collects my books, scooping them into his large hands. His eyes never deviate from my face.

My mouth goes dry as I stare at him. He's even more devastatingly handsome up close than he is in photos. Dark brows slash above his arresting eyes, giving him a severe, almost regal look. But little spots of gold in the amber soften the steely, unyielding intensity of his eyes, humanizing him.

There's something magnetic about him. I feel the pull deep in my core.

It's a dangerous feeling. He's destroyed more lives than I can count and fought more battles than I can even process.

Our fingers brush as he hands me the stack of books, and electricity arcs between us. It surges through my veins in a liquid rush, sending my heart rate galloping.

I fumble the books, nearly dropping them again, as I rise to my feet.

Jesus. Get it together, Brynna!

"Thank you," I manage, slightly breathless. I tuck an errant strand of hair behind my ear with a shaky hand, trying to pull myself together. I've dealt with men like him before. This one is no different.

It feels like a lie, even as I think it.

His full lips quirk in a half-smile. "The pleasure is all mine, *cariño*. It's not every day I literally run into such a beautiful woman."

He flirts as if he was born with charm dripping from his tongue... and I don't know what to do with that. Most men don't even try. They wouldn't dare cross my father to attempt it. But this one? Well, I think crossing my father is precisely what he intends.

And yet, despite the warning bells clanging in my head, I feel heat rising to my cheeks as he stands in front of me, cool and confident. My heart pounds a staccato rhythm against my ribs.

I need to get out of here.

I force a polite smile. "I appreciate your help, but I should be going..."

"What's the rush, *dulzura*?" He cocks his head, studying me intently. "I don't even know your name yet."

Right. As if he doesn't know exactly who I am.

The air crackles with tension as I stare at him, trying to decide how to respond.

"I suppose you found your way into a used bookstore right off campus completely by accident, then, Nazario?" I ask, arching a brow. "Because last I checked, UCLA didn't offer courses on becoming a Colombian drug lord."

Amusement flares in his gaze. "Ah, I see." That half-smile grows to a full-fledged grin. "And do they offer courses on being an Irish mob princess, *cariño*? Or are you the only one allowed to play by your rules here?"

"So you do know who I am," I mutter, refusing to take his bait. If there are any rules here, he's the one who knows them. I'm flailing in the dark. "Did you follow me here?"

"Follow you? No." His gaze flickers across my face. "Call it a happy coincidence. I was in need of new reading material."

"Right." I lick my suddenly dry lips. The man probably hasn't picked up a book in a decade. "Well, I have somewhere to be." Not technically a lie, though I'm in no rush to get there. "Thanks again."

I clutch my books to my chest like a shield and turn away. His deep chuckle follows me, setting tiny fires in my veins.

Halfway to the counter, his voice halts me. "Hey, Irish."

I glance over my shoulder to find him staring at me, his gaze smoldering.

"You're more suited to peace," he murmurs.

"What?"

"*War and Peace*." He nods at the stack of books in my hands. "Choose peace. It suits you better."

I blink wide eyes at him. "Have you ever thought about taking your own advice, Nazario?"

"Only every fucking day." He smirks at me, those amber eyes still locked on my face. "See you around, Irish."

I practically stumble over my own two feet as I make my way to the counter to check out, his gaze on me the entire time. I don't hear a word the cashier says to me as she bags up my books and then swipes my card before handing everything back to me. But I still feel the imprint of Nazario's scorching gaze between my shoulder blades as I hurry out of the store, my heart racing.

The man is a monster. My father would lose his mind if he knew that he'd been here.

And yet, when I glance back before stepping out onto the street and see him still standing there, watching me, the shiver that rips through me isn't entirely unpleasant. In fact, I like the way it feels almost as much as I like the savage hunger in his eyes. And I know I won't say a word.

Shit.

CHAPTER THREE

Naz

"*Príncipe*, wait."

I glance over my shoulder at Nicolas, one brow arched as impatience courses through me. "What is it?"

"Your ticket." He pulls it from his breast pocket with a grin, holding it out to me. "You'll need this if you plan to get into the gala."

I pause halfway out of the limo, muttering a soft curse. I didn't consider that I might need a ticket for this thing. Unlike Sullivan, I don't try to hide who I am by showing up for bullshit like this or throwing money at whatever cause is in at the moment. It's a ridiculous fucking thing to do, all things considered.

I'm a goddamn criminal. Why pretend to be anything other than who and what I am when everyone knows the truth? They knew about my family long before I was even old enough to comprehend that there are two different kinds of royalty in this world—and I'm not the right kind. And they feared me long before I understood there was anything to fear.

It's ironic, really. They'll take my money so long as I'm willing to hand it over. And they'll look the other way and pretend it isn't sprinkled with cocaine and dripping in blood while they line their pockets.

But as soon as I step inside that ballroom, the whispers will start. They don't want me here any more than I want to be here. My money is good enough for them. I'll never be accepted.

Too bad for them. Brynna Sullivan is inside. So tonight, they'll endure my company, regardless of how intolerable they find it. And I'll break out the checkbook, regardless of how distasteful I find it.

The fact that they're even willing to take money from motherfuckers like me or Nolan Sullivan isn't lost on me, however. Like I said, no one in this world is innocent. Everyone is guilty. I'm just more honest about my sins than most.

Tonight, Brynna is my sin. And I plan to sin like a motherfucker.

"Thank you," I murmur, plucking the ticket from Nicolas's hand before climbing from the limo. I straighten my jacket and stride forward, eager to set eyes on Sullivan's gorgeous daughter again.

Our meeting yesterday left me...unsettled. Actually, that's not true. I've been watching her for the last week. Every damn time I see her, I walk away with the same feeling.

She isn't what I expected. There's a grim brittleness to most of the women born in this world, a jaded cynicism that's impossible to miss. They're hard, as rotten at the core as the rest of us. There's nothing remotely jaded or cynical about Brynna. There's nothing grim, brittle, or rotten about her, either. She's soft and sweet, an innocent little lamb to the slaughter.

Fuck.

That innocence shouldn't make my cock ache the way it does.

I hand my ticket to the attendant at the door, not missing the way his eyes widen or the way his hand trembles as he accepts it.

He clears his throat, shifting nervously from one foot to the other. "Uh, enjoy your evening, Mr. Leyva."

I don't bother to respond, instead stepping past him into the ballroom. Crystal chandeliers spill golden light over opulent decor and gleaming marble floors. Massive flower arrangements scent the air, adding to the cloying mix of expensive perfume and cologne. It's fucking ridiculous. They're here to support a charity, yet they waste thousands just to surround themselves in luxury while they do it.

Every head turns in my direction, conversation faltering all across the ballroom as the Who's Who of Los Angeles society catches sight of me. Fear ripples through the crowd in an audible hum.

I smirk, amused by their discomfort, as I stride deeper into the room. They part like the Red Sea, not even daring to make eye contact. The fucking cowards. Most of them didn't make their millions any more honestly than I did. They just prefer to hide their misdeeds beneath a layer of forced civility. They shake hands, smile, and play this game when they'd stab anyone in this room in the back just as easily as I would.

It's a fucking joke.

Why bother with it when you're untouchable? Every law enforcement agency from here to Colombia knows what waits if I fall. Felipe Rojas will sweep across this hemisphere like a plague. Once his people are in, there will be no getting him out again.

He'll pour his poison into every corner of the world, carving out a kingdom for himself. That's what he wants—not just my cocaine fields. Not just to be the only drug baron in Colombia. He wants to be the only one, period.

Sometimes, the devil you know is preferable to the devil who'd kill you all. And Felipe Rojas? He's a murderous prick with horns the size of Texas. There are no rules where he's concerned.

And I'm the only thing holding him at bay. The blood on my hands doesn't even compare to what he's capable of doing—to the things he's already done. The FBI knows it. So does every other three letter agency in existence.

But the motherfuckers in this ballroom? Men no better than me despite the lies they tell themselves when their heads hit the fucking pillow? They look at me like I'm the goddamn devil.

It's laughable.

I scan the crowd, picking out those who don't shy away from my gaze. Nolan and Niall Sullivan hold court near the bar, both in tailored tuxes that cost more than most people make in a year. They stare coldly before shifting their gazes away. Eamon Callahan, the other major player in the Irish mob, isn't far away, already red-faced from too much Jameson. The man drinks like he gambles—and he's no better at the first than he is at the second.

Kieran and Granger Devlin, brothers who'd love to stick a blade in Eamon's throat, recline against a wall across the room, speaking with...I tense when I see their companion. Adrian Lombardi. Of course that prick would be here. He runs shit for the Italians on this coast, and they're all about appearances.

My jaw clenches, my blood heating. I can't fucking stand him. He's been a thorn in my side for years, one I'd very much like to snatch out and grind beneath my boot. Unfortunately, it isn't in the cards tonight.

I came for one reason and one reason only.

Where is she?

My balls ache as I scan the ballroom, noting every exit and potential threat, while I search. Nolan Sullivan may like to pretend he plays by the same rules the rest of these motherfuckers do, but I'm not naive. He'd put a bullet in my head without hesitation if given half a chance. I don't intend to make it easy for him.

I'm not here for him either, though. I'm here for *her*.

My gaze skirts across the room again, searching out alabaster skin, crimson hair, and those perceptive, striking emerald eyes.

I'm not leaving this bullshit event until I get my hands on Brynna Sullivan and...

I go still.

My pulse stutters as my eyes land on her, a sudden clench low in my gut sending a shiver of anticipation through me.

Dio. She's breathtaking.

She looks like a goddamn *princesa*, something out of a fairytale. Her ballgown hugs her ample curves, the emerald green bringing out the striking color of her eyes. I want to fist my hands in the fabric, feel it tear beneath my fingers as I expose her creamy skin inch by inch.

Would she whimper? Beg me to stop?

Cristo, I bet she'd look so fucking sweet with my hand around her throat, gasping for breath while she gushed all over my cock.

Her fiery hair is piled up on top of her head in an elegant bun, exposing the graceful column of her throat. My mouth goes dry as I imagine my lips there, tasting her, feeling her pulse fluttering wildly against my tongue.

She laughs at something her brother says, but it doesn't reach her eyes. I've seen her real smile, and this isn't it. This is the same fake smile she reserves for the world—for people who don't understand her or what she wants or needs. It's a show designed to ensure people look no further than the surface.

Her real smile is incredible. When she's happy—truly happy—she fucking glows. She was glowing in that bookstore today while she browsed through the stacks, her fingers trailing over the spines of books I doubt anyone in this room has ever read. But those books bring her to life. I think being away from her family does, too.

Niall leans in, whispering something in her ear with an affectionate grin. Whatever it is has her stiffening in offense, the lights in her eyes dimming further.

Anger flows through me, hot and vicious, at the sight. What did that prick say to her? How does he not notice how carelessly he hurts her?

I'm moving before I even give myself the command, shouldering my way through the crowd. I ignore the whispers that pop up in my wake, the wide eyes and frightened squawks. They mean nothing to me. But fuck it. If they want to talk, I'll give them a show.

It's what they really want anyway. For the goddamn god of war to entertain them, to prove that they're right about me. Spoiler alert: they are.

I keep my gaze locked on Brynna, drawn to her like a fucking lion to a lamb. She's the only bright spot in this entire shitshow of a gala...the only one deserving of actually being here.

And, for some reason, she's unhappy. I shouldn't care about that. But goddammit, I do.

Her father spots me first, pure hatred rolling through his expression as I approach. He places a hand on Brynna's elbow, a clear warning.

I smirk, truly amused for the first time since I arrived. If he didn't want me to touch his daughter, he should have kept his fucking hands away from my business. The bastard doesn't scare me. I've faced far worse than Nolan Sullivan and lived to tell the tale.

"Leyva," he says, his voice hard. "I don't recall seeing your name on the guest list tonight."

"Last minute decision," I murmur, my gaze locked on Brynna. She's staring at me, too, her expression flickering between wariness, curiosity, and frustration. It annoys her that she's intrigued by me, I think. *Cute.* "I thought it was time I put in an appearance at one of these things. I have to say, I'm underwhelmed by the guest list." I flick my gaze in his direction. "But then, I've heard you make a habit of attending these, don't you?"

Niall bristles at the insult, but Nolan simply laughs, a deep, humorless sound. "Careful, Leyva. People might think you're envious of what you don't have."

We both know he isn't talking about the reputation to attend these events. He means my goddamn shipping company, the bastard.

"People love to talk, Sullivan. As a matter of fact, we can't have people wondering why you're talking to me, now can we? What would they think?" I flash him a grin full of teeth. It's a promise and a threat all rolled into one. "I'd like to request a dance with your lovely daughter. She should be shown off, not kept hidden in a corner."

Nolan and Niall immediately stiffen, outrage painted across their faces. As expected, they don't make a move to stop me, though. With everyone watching us without trying to seem like they're watching us, these two are too worried about appearances to protect her as they should. In the dark, they'd strike without hesitation. But here, they're too fucking cowardly to do it.

She's a lamb to the slaughter in their care.

I hold out my hand to her, an unspoken challenge in my eyes.

Take it, little one. Come with me.

Her gaze drops to my outstretched hand before flicking back up to mine. A heartbeat passes. And then two. To my surprise, she slips her hand into mine, her skin soft.

I suppress a groan at the contact, a slow burn igniting in my veins. Fuck. This woman may be the death of me. But goddamn, what a way to go.

"Brynna," Nolan says tightly, the muscle in his jaw ticking. "What do you think you're doing?"

She turns to him, her expression serene even as her hand tightens around mine. "It's okay, Dad. It's just a dance."

"Yes, Sullivan," I agree, smirking at him. "It's just a dance. We wouldn't want anyone to think you had business with me, now would we?"

I don't give him a chance to respond before I lead her away, relishing the feel of her body brushing against mine with every step. She follows me willingly, her heels clicking against the marble tiles as I lead her toward the dance floor.

"Do you actually want to dance, little one?" I lean down, placing my lips near her ear.

She shivers at the question, hesitates, and then shakes her head. "No. I hate dancing at these things." That confession shakes on her lips, making my fucking blood roar in my veins.

As soon as the crowd swallows us, cutting us off from Sullivan's view, I cut across the edge of the dance floor, heading toward one of the terraces instead.

We step out, leaving the crowded ballroom and the watchful eyes of her father and brother behind. Out here, it's just us. The way it should be.

Cool night air swirls around us, making her shiver. I don't think she's cold, though. She's nervous.

"You look beautiful tonight, *dulzura,*" I tell her, drinking her in. Even in the dim light, she's radiant. Fucking hell. I don't think anyone has ever stolen my breath the way she does. "But then, you always do."

"We shouldn't be out here, Nazario," she says.

"Naz."

"What?"

"Call me Naz, little one."

"We shouldn't be out here, Naz. People will talk."

"You're right." I release her hand, instantly missing the warmth of it against mine, and step closer. She doesn't back away, instead holding her ground as I invade her space. Good girl. "People will talk. They always do, little one. But I thought you could use an escape. You don't seem thrilled to be here."

"I'm not," she says frankly. "But we do what we must." Her gaze flits across my face. "I think you probably understand how that feels."

"I do." A little too fucking well most days.

"Why are you here?"

Because you're here.

"What did your brother say to you?" I ask instead of telling her that particular truth.

Her brows furrow with confusion. "What?"

"He upset you. What did he say?"

"What are you talking about?"

"Before I came over," I murmur, watching her face intently. "He whispered something to you that upset you. What was it?"

"How do you..." she trails off, her eyes locking on my face as understanding dawns. "You were watching me."

"Everyone in the ballroom was watching you, *dulzura.* It's impossible not to notice you. What did he say?"

"Just something thoughtless," she says dismissively. "He says a lot of thoughtless things trying to be funny, Naz."

"What was it this time?"

"That my dress would fit better if I hadn't taken so long picking out my stupid books yesterday," she mumbles, glancing away from me as her cheeks turn pink.

That fucking prick. Rage surges through me in a vicious black cloud. I want to wrap my hands around his throat and choke the breath from him. So slowly he feels every agonizing second.

She's clearly uncomfortable being here already, and he decided to make it worse, saying some bullshit like that? She deserves far better. The dress isn't a problem. Neither is she. She's a goddamn *princesa* making my cock hard just by existing.

Niall Sullivan's mouth is the totality of the fucking problem.

"The dress fits you like a dream, Brynna," I say softly, no hint of anger in my voice. That, I reserve for her brother. "You look like a true *princesa*. I haven't been able to take my eyes off you since I walked through the doors." I run my hand down her arm, fascinated by the way gooseflesh rises in response. "I haven't been able to keep you out of my head all day."

"What do you want from me, Nazario?" she asks, her voice steady despite the rapid rise and fall of her chest. I hear the hint of vulnerability in her voice, though. It's raw, an old wound she desperately doesn't want to expose to me.

"You know what I want."

"Right." Her lips compress into a thin, disapproving line. "A pawn to use against my father."

The way she says it leaves no doubt that she's been down that road before. How many times? How many men have tried to put their hands on her to get to her father? The thought makes me murderous. And maybe it makes me honest, too.

"I don't want a pawn, little one." I reach out again, trailing a fingertip along the line of her collarbone. My cock throbs at the contact. Fuck, the things I want to do to this girl. Would she let me if she knew? Would she beg for me to stuff my cock down her pretty little throat until her eyes watered? "I want you."

She shivers at my touch, taking a step away from me. "I'm not yours to take, Naz."

"Not yet," I agree, sliding my hand up to cup her cheek. "But you will be."

"No, I won't," she says. "Whatever is between you and my father is between you and my father. I won't be a pawn."

"I told you that I'm not interested in a pawn. I'm interested in you in my bed. You, wrapped around me." I brush my thumb over her bottom lip. "You, lost in pleasure so intense you can't breathe through it. I want to fuck you open and make you scream, Brynna."

Her lips part, a hot retort forming, but I silence her with my thumb on her bottom lip. "Don't fight it, *dulzura*. I see the way you look at me. I feel the way you tremble when I touch you. You want the same things I do."

She stares at me, conflict warring in her eyes. But I see the desire, the longing, the same hunger lashing at me. I see the fear and distrust, too. I don't think she fears me, though. She fears the consequences of putting her trust in me. She fears letting herself want me.

I chafe at it even as I understand it. She's a smart girl to doubt a monster. But this monster? Well, it's fucking complicated. And getting more so by the minute.

Because there's something about this girl that has me all twisted into knots. This should be simple, easy. Her father fucked with my business, so I break her to teach him a lesson. And yet...this has nothing to do with him. It has nothing to do with business. It has everything to do with her and the way she looks at me like I'm a puzzle she wants to solve.

For once, I want to be solved. I want to let her unravel all my secrets, come what may.

What the fuck is that about? I don't know, but I don't entirely hate it, either.

"I can't," she whispers reluctantly, but she doesn't pull away.

"You can. You will. Because you're mine, Brynna." I lean in, brushing my lips across the corner of her mouth. I flick my tongue against it, stealing a tiny taste of her. "And I protect what's mine."

Her soft gasp lands against my lips, turning my cock to stone. I pull back, meeting her gaze. The uncertainty is still there, but so is the fire. The defiance.

Goddamn, it's beautiful.

"I belong to no one," she growls, lifting her chin. "Least of all to you, Nazario."

I grin, savage and proud. *Cristo*. She's incredible.

"One day soon, you're going to ask me to claim every piece of you, *dulzura*. You'll beg me to fucking break you, and you'll want it more than air. When you do, I'll give you the fucking world." I step back, putting distance between us before I drag her into my arms and kiss the fire from her lips. She's not ready for that yet. But soon.

"You should get back to your father before he comes looking for you. But we'll be seeing each other again soon." I pause, my gaze running over her. "Don't let anyone put their hands on you, Irish. I won't allow them to keep them if they do."

With that, I turn and stride away, leaving her standing on the terrace, her outraged gaze burning into my back.

I chuckle to myself.

Her thoughts are so loud, I practically hear them screaming at me. But I don't turn around. I let her watch, let her wonder...let the anticipation build. Because when she finally crumbles into my arms, victory will be all that much sweeter.

And when that day comes?

Not even the armies of hell will be able to stop me from claiming her as mine. Her father certainly won't.

Cristo. What am I thinking?

She won't ever be mine.

She's supposed to be a means to an end, a piece to move across the board. I should be leaving with her on my arm, reminding her father what happens when you fuck with me. And yet...

The thought of spoiling her, of tainting her light with my darkness, fills me with a sense of dread I've never experienced before.

Fuck.

I glance over my shoulder at her as I reach the door, my breath catching in my throat as I see her fingertips pressed against her cheek, a look of wonder and confusion on her face.

I groan softly.

I can lie to myself all I want, but the writing is on the wall. Brynna Sullivan stopped being a means to an end before I ever stepped foot in that fucking bookstore yesterday. Whatever this is...it has nothing to do with her father. I'm not sure it ever did.

I want her in my arms and in my bed. Fuck her father. Fuck our war. It's irrelevant.

I stride back into the ballroom, my mind reeling. The air feels charged, electric. I can still feel the softness of her skin beneath my lips, hear the way she gasped when I kissed her.

I need a fucking drink.

I make my way to the bar, signaling for a shot of tequila. The bartender pours a glass, sliding it across the polished wood toward me.

I snatch the glass with a shaking hand and down it in one gulp, savoring the burn as it slides down my throat. It doesn't silence the roar in my mind. It doesn't even slow it.

"Drowning your sorrows, Leyva?" a familiar voice drawls from behind me.

I tense and turn, coming face to face with Adrian Lombardi. He's leaning against the bar, an arrogant smirk playing on his lips.

"Lombardi," I mutter, my tone cold. "I didn't know they let trash into these events."

His jade eyes flash with anger, but his smile doesn't budge. "Careful, Leyva. You don't want to start something you can't finish with all these people watching."

I laugh, a harsh, humorless sound, as I set my empty glass on the bar. Has everyone forgotten who the fuck I am? Or are they all really this fucking eager for a show?

"I always finish what I start, Lombardi. Remember that," I mutter, turning to leave.

His next comment stops me in my tracks before I even make it two steps.

"Sullivan's daughter is a pretty little thing, isn't she?"

I go still, rage simmering through my veins. "Watch your fucking mouth."

He chuckles, a mocking smirk curving his lips up at the corners. "Did I hit a nerve, Leyva? Interesting. Maybe I will ask her to dance, see what it is about her that has you so riled up."

Before he can even blink, I have him by the throat, slamming him up against the bar. Stools get knocked aside, landing upside down. A glass bottle shatters, sending scotch and glass raining down around us.

The room goes silent, everyone turning to stare.

"Listen to me carefully," I say, my voice deadly calm. "If you so much as look in her fucking direction, they won't ever find your fucking body. Do you understand me?"

Lombardi just smirks, even as his face turns a satisfying shade of purple.

I hold him for a moment longer before I release him, stepping back. "You're lucky there are witnesses, you prick."

"Always a pleasure taunting you, Leyva," he says, laughing hoarsely.

I smile, cold and vicious. "Oh, this is the last time you do it. Trust me on that, *pendejo*."

I turn and stalk out of the ballroom, leaving him standing there. The crowd parts before me again, completely silent as I pass through. But as soon as I do, whispers follow in my wake.

Fuck it, though, right? They wanted fucking *Dios de la Guerra* to put on a show, so let them talk. Now, they know what happens when someone threatens what belongs to me.

And Brynna is mine, even if she doesn't know it yet. I will burn this city to ash and ruin before I let anyone take her from me.

CHAPTER FOUR

Brynna

"Where the fuck have you been?" Niall clamps a hand down on my arm as soon as I step back inside the ballroom, his grip like iron. "I've been looking everywhere for you."

"I stepped out for some air," I mutter, tugging discreetly against his hold as people glance in our direction. It's not technically a lie. "Is that a crime?"

His dark scowl tells me that, apparently, it is a crime. I'm supposed to be a good little girl and do as I'm told. Except...I don't feel like playing that role tonight. I haven't felt like playing it in years. He and my father have yet to notice.

"What did he want?" Niall demands.

"To piss you off?" I shrug, my heart hammering against my ribcage as I try to wriggle my way out of telling him the truth. "Judging by the look on your face, I'd say it worked, wouldn't you?"

Niall's dark glower grows even darker. Impressive, honestly.

"Can you let go of my arm now, or do you plan to drag me through the gala like a recalcitrant child? Everyone is already."

I'm not kidding about that. Everyone in the general vicinity is focused on us, leaning in as if trying to hear what we're discussing. Because of Naz? Do I even need to ask? Of course it's because of Naz.

He strolled through the doors, set his sights on me, and set the entire place on fire with rumors and speculation.

"Shit." My brother immediately releases his hold on me, his expression softening with regret. For all his flaws, he isn't a bad man. He's a complicated one. A criminal, yes. A hedonist, absolutely. A pain in my ass, only every day of the week. But he means well. He worries. I guess he has plenty of reason for that. "I'm sorry. I'm an asshole. Did I hurt you?"

"No." I pause for a beat. "But you are getting on my nerves."

A tiny smile flickers at his lips. "So Naz didn't do any damage, then?" He scrutinizes my expression, genuine worry in his gaze. "You're okay?"

"I'm fine, Niall." I roll my eyes, guilt flickering through me. I hate that I'm lying even as I do it...but I do it anyway. "Honestly, you worry too much. What was he going to do in a room full of witnesses? He wanted to annoy you and Dad. He succeeded. As soon as he accomplished his mission, he disappeared."

I'm no longer sure that's what he wants at all. He meant it when he said he wants me. I'm just not entirely sure *why* he wants me so badly. The rational half of my brain screams that it's exactly what I suspect—I'm some pawn in whatever game he's playing with my father. But the other half rebels against the thought. That half, stupidly, wants a reason to trust him. It wants a reason to fall into whatever this fascination is. It wants to believe he wants me simply for me.

The way he looks at me is electric, pulsing with something I've never felt. I like it a little too much. And that's dangerous. *He's* dangerous—and I don't mean for obvious reasons.

I'm trying to carve out a little independence for myself. He's a threat to that in far too many ways. If I tell my brother that he kissed me, it'll fan the flames of war. And if I tell Niall that I liked it?

Well, I'll never see the light of day again. He and my father will have me surrounded by guards before I can even blink. No more freedom, no more school, no more tiny little life outside of their world.

Everything I've fought for will disappear, and I'll be trapped like a rat in a cage all over again. It's not a risk I'm willing to take when I only just slipped out of my cage. Whatever Naz wants...I just have to ensure he doesn't get it.

Doubt swirls through me for the thousandth time since he left me standing on the terrace. He's...alluring. Tempting in a way that's terrifying.

And I've never been good at resisting temptation.

It's precisely why I had to have this damn dress fitted yesterday when it fit fine six months ago.

Niall snorts. "As if he's capable of slinking off without causing problems."

My brows furrow. "What does that mean?"

"He got into a fight with Adrian Lombardi before he stormed out."

"He got into a fight?" I blink wide eyes, startled. "Why? When?"

"Five minutes ago." Niall nods toward the bar. I follow his gaze, watching in shock as a member of the waitstaff sweeps broken glass into a dustpan while another straightens overturned barstools. "No idea what it was about. 'Da is talking to Adrian, trying to sort it out, see if he can find anything useful."

"Useful?" I glance back at my brother, my brow furrowing.

He shoots me a smirk, his eyes glittering with intent. "Do you really think we're going to let him get away with what he did tonight, *deirfiúr*? No one messes with you, least of all Nazario fucking Leyva."

My stomach churns, anxiety pulsing through me. This is exactly what I don't want. Why is this world always tit for tat, you hurt me, so I hurt you? It's fucking exhausting.

"It was just a dance, Niall," I say quietly. "He didn't do anything. He was a perfect gentleman."

"Right." Niall snorts. "As if the prick even knows the definition."

"Niall!" I glower at him. "I'm serious. He didn't do anything. He was nice to me. That's it." I glance back toward the bar, away from my brother. "He said he liked my dress."

"Jesus Christ," Niall growls, spinning me around to face him with a hand on my arm. "You like him."

"What? No, of course not," I lie hastily, pasting an innocent look on my face—the same one he and my father never bother to look past. Just like they never look past the fake smiles and false reassurance that I'm perfectly fine, fine, fine. Managing them is second nature at this point. It's all I've done for years. And frankly, it's exhausting.

I'm tired of being the perfect little princess who does as she's told and has no dreams beyond placating her overprotective family. I'm tired of pretending I was ever her to begin with. I'm just...not. I want *more*.

Maybe I'm not doing as good a job managing my brother as I thought because his emerald eyes narrow on my face, his gaze assessing. "You know you can talk to me, right?" he says softly.

Ha. Not about this, I can't. If I tell him the truth, he'll lose his mind. Family is everything to Niall. And the fact that I liked the way it felt when one of the family's biggest enemies had his hands on me? Well, he'll never understand that.

"I know," I say instead of telling him any of that. "But there's nothing to talk about, Niall. Nazario was trying to get a rise out of you and Dad, and it clearly worked. But he was nice to me, and I appreciated it. It was a refreshing change from the way these little power struggles usually go." I shoot him a pointed glance. "Would you prefer another kidnap attempt?"

"Jesus," he growls, a storm roiling in his eyes. "Don't even joke about that, Brynna."

"I'm not," I say softly. "I'm just pointing out that, all things considered, asking me to dance was the least of what he could have done. We've been there before."

Niall mutters a curse, scrubbing a shaking hand down his face, and I feel like a jerk for even bringing it up. But I'm right, and he can't deny that. We've been down that road before. It's the only reason I bite my tongue when he and our father are so overbearingly overprotective. The target painted on my back hasn't grown any smaller over the years. I've just gotten better at avoiding it.

"Can we get out of here now?" I ask quietly. "I'd really, really like to get out of these shoes."

"Fuck, yes." Niall drops his hand back to his side, jerking his chin in a nod. "Let's go."

I exhale a relieved breath, following behind him as he forges a path through the crowd for me. I don't miss the way they watch me go. Nor do I miss their whispers. Niall may believe what I said about Naz, but these people clearly don't.

Thanks to his attention, the target on my back is now bigger than ever. Lovely.

"What are you reading?"

I glance up from my book to find my father standing at the door to my room, still dressed in the tux he wore to the gala. He looks out of place among the lacy throw pillows and pale purple fabrics, like an aging warrior.

"*War and Peace.*" I roll onto my back and then sit upright. "Did you just get home?"

"Mmhmm." He steps into my room. "*War and Peace*, huh? What do you think?"

"I've read it before," I say quietly, placing my bookmark between the pages to mark my spot. "It's fascinating."

"I always thought so, too." He leans against the wall. "*One must be cunning and wicked in this world*," he quotes softly.

Of course that's the line that resonates with him. He's both of those things. In spades.

"*We love people not so much for the good they've done us, but as for the good we've done them*," I retort, making him smile.

"You always have seen the world far more like your mother did than like me or your brother do." His eyes crinkle at the corners. "You keep the two of us honest."

Is there honesty in what they do? I'm not sure. But my father isn't a bad man any more than my brother is. He's just a man. And like most men, he's full of flaws. But he's not entirely flawed. I know he loves me and Niall. He'd do anything for us. And I know he does what he can to balance the scales, to put just as much good into the world as he does bad. Does guilt drive him? Perhaps. But at least he tries.

Does Naz? For some reason, I think he plays by a different set of rules entirely. He lives by his own code. I'm just not entirely sure what that code is.

"How was the rest of the gala?" I ask my father, trying to distract myself. It's late, I'm tired, and a certain Colombian drug lord has occupied far too much of my mind already tonight.

I've thought myself in circles, trying to sort out why he's so fascinating to me. And I've come up with nothing but a lingering headache.

"It was fine." My father's brows furrow as he stares at me. "That's what I want to talk to you about."

Great. I should have known I wasn't going to get away without a conversation about Naz with him, too.

"Are you all right, Brynna?" he asks, unable to hide the worry in his eyes.

"I'm perfectly fine, Dad," I sigh. "It was just a dance."

How many more times am I going to have to tell that particular lie before I manage to convince myself that what happened tonight meant nothing?

"Are you sure? You know you can talk to me, right?"

"I'm positive." I force a bright smile and lie to him, exactly like I lied to Niall. "Nazario was polite. We danced. He complimented my dress. And then I went outside to get some air and he did whatever Nazario does. That's it."

He studies me in silence for several long moments. He seems troubled, as if there's far more going on here than I know. "Perhaps we should reconsider letting you roam campus alone. At least for a little while."

I carefully set my book aside, trying to stay calm as my heart thuds against my breastbone. "You promised you wouldn't do that."

"I know." Guilt flickers in his gaze. "But things have changed."

"Because Nazario asked me to dance?" I cross my arms, scowling at him. "Like I told Niall, he only did it to get under your skin. And it clearly worked if you're trying to change our agreement about college now. I'm twenty-one, not twelve. I don't need a bodyguard just to get a freaking education."

"No, not because of the dance," he says, his gaze locked on my face. "Because Leyva attacked Lombardi after he mentioned that he might ask you to dance."

"I..." I stutter, caught off guard. "I'm sure I had nothing to do with it. The last time I was forced to deal with Adrian Lombardi, I considered resorting to violence, too. He tends to bring out that quality in most people."

The man is an infuriating monster. He doesn't care about anyone or anything but himself. My father knows this just as well as I do. He's wanted to hit him a time or two himself.

Crap. Did Naz really attack him because he suggested dancing with me? Doubtful. He's too controlled for that. But did Lombardi say something about me to provoke Naz into attacking him? Probably.

What was it Naz said before he walked away?

Don't let anyone put their hands on you, Irish. I won't allow them to keep them if they do.

This is...not good. It's not good at all. And judging by the look on my father's face, he isn't buying my explanation, either. He knows Naz is up to something.

"Nazario is dangerous, *A stór*," he says quietly. "He lies as easily as he breathes. He'll tell you a pretty story and then destroy you just to punish me."

"Punish you for what?" I ask. "What did you do that has the two of you on the verge of war?"

"It doesn't matter," he says wearily, pushing away from the wall. "What matters is you and your brother." He swallows, worry burning bright in his eyes. "I promised your mother to keep you both safe. But Niall is too fucking much like me, *A stór*. I can't stop him from putting himself in harm's way. I can't risk anything happening to you, however. She'd never forgive that."

"Dad," I say softly, my heart clenching in a vise. Even now, a decade later, he still mourns her. "Nothing is going to happen to me."

"Promise me that you'll stay away from Leyva, Brynna," he demands, reaching out to stroke my hair like he always did when I was a little girl. "Help an old man rest easy."

"Of course I'll stay away from Nazario Leyva." The promise scalds my tongue as it spills from my lips, searing into my mind with agonizing clarity. *Stay away from Nazario Leyva.* It's such a simple vow, and yet it feels like a betrayal—of myself, of the inexplicable pull I feel toward him, of the electric thrill that raced through me when he had his hands on my body, his amber eyes boring into mine.

But I force the words out anyway. Because disappointing my father, worrying him further after everything our family has been through, is impossible.

I'm still trapped in the facade of that perfect little princess. And I'm the one holding the damn doors of my cage closed.

But when my father smiles, I smile back, pretending that promise didn't hurt at all, that every cell in my body didn't rebel against giving it. I smile until he strolls out, confident that I'll be his obedient little daughter and keep my word.

I'm not nearly as confident. I think Naz may have embedded himself into my very being with the brush of his lips against mine tonight, stamping his dark temptation so deeply into my psyche that nothing will ever get him out again now.

And I don't have the first clue what to do about that.

CHAPTER FIVE

Naz

Nicolas was right. Someone on my payroll is a fucking rat. There's no denying it as I pour over the financial data spread across the top of my desk, scanning every detail. It doesn't add up.

I drum my fingers against the mahogany surface, my frustration growing as I pick out details that don't match. The Garcia account is missing two grand; the Alvarez shipment was off by a kilo. Another three grand is missing from the Bandari Fund. Someone is stealing from me.

Who? I mentally run through a list, trying to figure out who the fuck has a death wish.

Josef? Andrés? Camilo? Griffin? Aside from Nicolas, they're the four I trust most. Would any of the four betray me? Would they throw in with Rojas? With Sullivan?

Someone has.

This is precisely why I trust no one. Motherfuckers *can't* be trusted. They'll smile in your goddamn face while shoving a knife between your ribs. In this world, it's kill or be killed. And no one is fucking loyal.

I push back from my desk and stalk over to the floor-to-ceiling windows overlooking downtown LA, cursing under my breath. Bright sunlight filters over the city below, reflecting off the cool blue water...softening it. It's a lie, though. Between the gangs, the mobs, and motherfuckers like me, this city is always on the brink of all-out war. It's just a powder keg ready to blow.

I can relate. I feel caged, murderous rage simmering just below the surface. I want to put my fist through someone's skull. Hunt down whoever betrayed me and paint the walls with their blood. Fucking desecrate their bones.

But I can't do that. Until I know every last detail of what they're doing, who is involved, and why, I need be logical, precise. But once I have all the pieces? I'll rip the fucking cancer from this organization with my own hands. No one will cross me again.

Cristo. I need to hit something. Break something. Fucking destroy.

Lombardi. I've been meaning to slit his miserable throat for days. Might as well put all this rage to use handling that situation.

No. I need to see her first.

I haven't set eyes on her in four days. I've been here, letting the anticipation build, letting her miss me...slowly going out of my goddamn mind.

I'm a cord pulled too taut, ready to snap.

I stride back to the desk, snatching my keys from the top before stalking from my office. The door slams behind me hard enough to rattle the frame.

Nicolas glances up from his desk, brows furrowing. "*Príncipe*?"

"I have something to do," I snap, not stopping to explain. "Call if anything comes up."

"Will do, *príncipe*."

I start to storm away and then stop, wheeling around to face him. "I want the names of everyone on our payroll on my desk come morning."

His brows widen. "Eh, that may take some time, Naz. You have people all over the place."

"Make it happen, Nicolas," I grit out. "Every name. And either find the motherfucker running information to Sullivan, or I'm going to start culling people from the ranks myself. Every last one of them if that's what it takes."

"*Príncipe*," he protests, shock filtering through his expression. "Half of them have been with you for a decade.

They're loyal only to you. We'll find the ones who aren't. I just need a little time, yes?"

"Yeah, well, you're out of time, Nicolas. Find them. Now," I snarl, beyond being placated. If he doesn't find them, I will. If I have to cut through every corner of this organization to do it, that's what I'll do. But I want them found now, before they do more damage.

I storm through the office, my footsteps echoing on the floor. My people scatter out of my way as if they sense the black cloud hanging over me. Smart choice. Anyone stupid enough to get caught in my way might not like the consequences today.

I treat my people well and pay generously for their loyalty. People may think the worst of me, but I'm not a total fucking monster. I actually have a goddamn soul. And I care about everyone I employ. I may not be puppies and rainbows about it, but I protect what's mine. They've always been mine. But today? Well, I just had an abject fucking lesson in how far their loyalty extends to me. And it's not that far, apparently.

I mutter a curse, slamming my finger against the elevator button. Jesus Christ, I need to get out of here.

Thirty-three minutes later, I street park near the School of Law and cut across Shapiro Courtyard to Dodd Hall, long, ground-eating strides carrying me closer with every beat of my heart. Fuck. I just need to set eyes on her. Just a single glimpse to settle the rage rattling around inside me like a demon.

I know it's a lie, even as I repeat it to myself. If I see her, I'll approach her. I'll put my hands on her again. I won't be able to stop myself. She's in my blood now, pumping through my veins like a drug.

Ironic, considering I've never used the fucking things. I supply them to the dealers who do. It's always been one of my rules. Don't be fucking stupid and use your own goddamn product. Rules are necessary in this world. They've kept me alive and one step ahead of Rojas since I took the reins at sixteen, a full fucking decade ago now.

But I seem to be smashing through every single one of them for Brynna Sullivan.

Don't think with your dick? Too late. Don't get close? My motherfucking bad. Don't get involved? Already did it. Don't catch feelings? Well, goddamn. Is that what I'm doing here? Catching feelings?

Is that even a question?

I stroll around the side of Dodd Hall, intending to take up a position in the courtyard to wait for her class to let out...but I don't get that far. As soon as I step around the side of the building, my eyes lock on her alabaster skin and crimson hair. She's sitting on the steps, her face tipped up to the sun.

I pause midstep, devouring the sight of her. *Dio*. She's a vision, an angel bathed in sunlight. It spills across her skin, making her almost glow.

The rage inside me dies in an instant, the inferno extinguished by something equally as potent but far softer. Affection. Desire. Longing. All three surge through my veins as I stare at her.

The sight of her always hits me hard, but now? After four endless days? It's like coming up for air after being submerged in the darkest depths of this world.

Her hair tumbles around her shoulders in wild crimson waves, like flames dancing in the light. It looks so fucking soft. My fingers ache to slip into it, to wrap the strands around my fist as I claim her perfect pink mouth.

She looks so goddamn innocent and pure, completely untouched by the darkness of my world. And something about that purity makes me ache to put my filthy hands all over her, to claim that innocence as my own. To defile her in every way possible.

But I don't want to destroy that innocence. I want to possess it, to preserve it.

To fucking worship it on my knees.

I stride forward, my cock throbbing against my zipper with every step. Halfway there, she dips her head, and her gaze locks with mine. For a fleeting moment, her expression is wide open to me, no walls between us.

I see excitement spark in the depths of her emerald eyes, as if she's happy to see me. Desire chases immediately after. And then she seems to remember that she isn't supposed to like me, isn't supposed to want me. She blinks a scowl into place, her lips pursing.

"You," she growls.

Fuck, she's cute when she's pretending she's fierce. Will she be so brave when I'm pinning her to the bed beneath me, driving into her so hard she thinks she's going to break?

"Hello, Irish," I drawl, my lips twitching. "Fancy meeting you here."

"What do you want this time, Naz?" she asks, exasperation coloring her tone. She doesn't even give me a chance to answer before she throws her hand up. "You know what? Don't answer that. I'm still looking over my shoulder from the last time you showed up and ruined my night."

My smile grows, the rage I felt driving over her a distant memory. "Ruined your night? I think you mispronounced enhanced your evening, *princesa*."

She rolls her eyes at me. "No, I said precisely what I intended to say. Why are you here this time?"

"Out for a stroll," I lie.

"Uh-huh, sure." She crosses her arms, pushing her breasts up in her little shirt. "Stalking isn't really a good look on you, Nazario. It screams desperate."

"For you?" I reach out, running a fingertip down an errant curl. It's exactly as soft as I imagined. "Always, *princesa*. I thought we were clear about that."

She sighs heavily. "What do you want, Naz?"

I consider teasing her further, only to realize I have no desire to do it. "My office was stifling," I murmur. "I needed fresh air and something soothing to look at before I did something I'm sure I'd regret eventually." My eyes bore into hers. "So...here I am."

She eyes me silently, the tip of her tongue caught between her teeth. "Do I even want to know what it is you were considering doing that you'd regret?"

"Murder. Mayhem. Monstrous acts." I shrug a shoulder. "Take your pick, little one."

She blinks at me, shivering. "Jesus, Naz."

"I won't lie to you," I murmur softly. "You know who and what I am. Denying it would be an insult to you, little one." I wrap her curl around my finger. "I'm not interested in insulting you."

"I...thank you," she whispers, her lashes fluttering. "It's nice to be treated like an adult instead of as a little girl who needs to be protected at all costs."

"Oh, I never said I wouldn't protect you." I untwist her hair from around my finger, brushing my knuckles across her cheek as I lean closer. "No one touches what belongs to me, *mi cielito*. I'll raze this city to the fucking ground if anyone tries. But you are all woman." My lips skim her cheek. "I should know. You've had my fucking cock hard since I set eyes on you the first time."

"Naz," she whispers, a warning in her tone. She doesn't lean away, though. Nor does she tell me to stop. She may not want to want me, but she does anyway.

"Run away with me for the day, *princesa*," I breathe against her skin. "Spend one afternoon with me."

"I..."

"Say yes, Brynna. You know it's what you want to do." My lips graze her cheek again, one hand around her thick waist. I don't give a fuck who sees us. It's unlikely we're the first to kiss on these steps. "I'll tell you anything you want to know."

She pulls back slightly, her eyes locking with mine. The avid curiosity burning in their depths makes my balls ache. *Dio*. Who is this girl that this carrot is the one that entices her? Not my money, not power, not sex, but knowledge of who I am. "Anything?"

"Anything," I agree, unable to resist touching my tongue to the corner of her lips. She shivers, her upper body swaying closer to me. "Whatever you want to know."

"Why did you hit Adrian Lombardi?" she asks, breathless.

Ah, so she heard about that, did she?

"He thought taunting me was a good choice." I flick my tongue against the corner of her lip again. "I disabused him of that notion."

"Taunted you how?" Her eyes are dark, her pupils blown wide. Fuck. I want to wrap her curls around my fist and taste every inch of that perfect mouth.

"He thought waking a sleeping giant was a good idea, *mi cielito*." My grip around her waist tightens, my fingers digging into her soft flesh.

"What did he say, Naz?"

"He mentioned putting his hands on you." I tip her head back, meeting her gaze. "What did I tell you about that, *princesa*?"

Her lips part, and I can't fucking take it anymore. I need to kiss her, need to taste that perfect mouth before I snap.

I dip my head, my mouth slanting down over hers. The first full brush of her lips against mine is pure bliss. It's not gentle or sweet. It's fierce, feral.

She gasps softly, and I take the opportunity to lick into her mouth, my tongue tangling with hers in a blatantly erotic claim of possession. The sound of her soft whimper shoots straight to my cock.

Dio. She tastes like fucking heaven—honey and sin and unschooled innocence. I've never felt anything this intense before, never had this soul-deep craving to possess and claim before.

I want to fucking devour her.

My hand curls around her nape, holding her in place as I plunder her mouth, branding her with my taste. Stealing hers.

She yields to me so sweetly, letting me take what I need. And I do, my tongue sliding against hers, stroking, caressing. Claiming.

Heat sears through my blood, desire steaming through my veins. I pour every ounce of frustrated desire and raw need into her, letting her feel every ounce of it.

She mewls into my mouth, her little hands fisting in my shirt as she clings to me. I nip at her bottom lip, and she shudders.

Fuck. The way she responds to me.

I want to destroy her with pleasure, shatter her into a million pieces, and then put her back together again. Throw her down on the steps and fuck her right here, in front of God and everyone, make sure they know she's mine.

I'm like a man possessed, lost to the perfect slide of her mouth against mine and the breathy little sounds she makes.

I force myself to pull back after a long moment, breathing hard.

Her eyes flutter open, glazed with lust and unfocused. She's as beautiful wrecked from my kiss now as she was looking like a *princesa* at the gala. Moreso because this is more her than that dress was.

She's stripped down to the most primal of instincts, breathless and aching. This is the side of her no one else ever sees, the one she hides from the world. It's Brynna, raw and real.

"Come with me," I whisper, my lips grazing the shell of her ear. "Give me one afternoon, *princesa*. We won't even leave campus if it's what you want."

She bites down on that kiss-swollen bottom lip, her eyes wide as they lock with mine. I see her inner conflict warring in their emerald depths, desire battling with good sense. She aches to say yes. I see it. I feel it in the way she arches into me, seeking more contact. More of my touch.

But she's struggling with the desire, a good girl to her core. The angel on her shoulder tells her to be smart, to stay the fuck away from me. But the devil on the other shoulder? He's whispering for her to take what she wants. To give in to the dark just this once.

In the end, the devil wins.

And I'm the motherfucking devil.

She exhales a breath, nodding as she slips her hand into mine. "Okay," she whispers. "But we're staying on campus. And I want something first."

"Name it," I growl, victory surging through my veins. I've won this war, and we both know it. She's mine now. She might not realize it yet, but it's only a matter of time before she surrenders every little piece of herself, body and fucking soul.

"Let Lombardi live."

"Why?"

She shrugs. "People shouldn't die just because they say something annoying, Naz. Not even someone who says annoying things as often as he does."

"Why, *princesa*?" I grit out, watching her face, searching for the truth. Whatever it is, it isn't that.

Her gaze drifts from mine, her teeth sinking into her bottom lip. "Maybe too many people have already died because of what they've said or done or tried to do to me," she finally whispers, a tremor in her voice. "And maybe I don't want his death on my conscience, too."

I guess that's clear enough, isn't it? And the answer is a fucking tragedy. She's innocent, her hands clean. But she carries guilt that doesn't belong to her anyway because, like the rest of us, she lives in this world, too.

"I won't kill him," I agree, incapable of adding to her burden when it's already heavier than she should have to carry.

CHAPTER SIX

Brynna

Naz takes me back to the old bookstore right off campus, where we first met. As we step through the glass-fronted door, the familiar, comforting smell of cracked leather and dusty pages swirls around me, settling my nerves.

The bell jangles, and the pretty blonde cashier glances in our direction.

Recognition flares in her eyes as she notices Naz at my side. A healthy dose of fear parades across her face.

Does everyone in this city know him on sight?

God, probably. His picture has been plastered all over the papers for as long as I can remember. He's more talked about around here than most celebrities, as notorious as the most reckless and wild of them. Only, the respect he's earned is the kind most people don't want—the kind we reserve for the boogeyman, for the childish flights of fancy that enthrall and fascinate us even as they terrify us.

We tiptoe to the closet and peer in, both terrified and full of awe, praying we don't wake the beast slumbering within...but desperate to see if he's really in there anyway. We want to glimpse him, even as we're afraid of casting our eyes upon him. We respect him and his boundaries because we know that if we don't, he'll destroy us. Gobble us up like those little pigs in a straw house.

That's Naz. The monster in the closet. The big, bad wolf.

And he has his fingers laced through mine, stroking my thumb as if we're just some ordinary couple, here to pick out something to read together.

I don't know what I'm doing. I don't know why I can't stop. And yet...I can't. Every moment I spend with him binds me more tightly to him. I'm prey, tangled in the web of a hunting spider. And somewhere along the way, I think I stopped struggling. I gave in to the inevitable, waiting for his poison to infect me. Quivering in anticipation of his strike.

He catches my gaze, winking as he flips the sign over the door to closed. The cashier watches him do it, not saying a word. Stop Nazario Leyva? She wouldn't dare.

But I'm not her. And for some reason, this wicked man has let me see beneath the monstrous scales he presents to the world. There's more to him than just the monster. He's not just the cocaine prince. He's...Naz. And I think that man is as conflicted and disoriented by the connection growing between us as I am. He's just as human as I am. He just hides it better.

"Naz," I mutter, frowning in disapproval. "You can't just close the store because you're here."

"I'm not, *princesa*." His striking eyes meet mine. "I'm closing it because you are."

My heart flutters at his casual sincerity, even though it shouldn't.

"They have a business to run," I protest.

"All will be well, *mi alma*." He cups my cheek, his fingertips gentle as they feather across my cheekbone. "I'll ensure the store doesn't suffer for the privacy I carve out for you." His lips brush the shell of my ear. "You don't want your father to find out about us. I'm trying to ensure I follow your rules."

My father. It's a grim reminder of exactly what's at stake here, of exactly what I'm risking. I made a promise. I've spent the last four days wrestling with myself, trying like hell to convince myself to keep it. And as soon as Naz appeared, all of that inner turmoil meant exactly nothing. Precisely like I feared it would.

This man is dangerous to everything I'm trying to build for myself, exactly like I knew he would be. And yet, I'm here anyway, allowing him to pull me deeper into the store, my hand laced in his. And yet...I still taste the sin of his kiss, feel the electric heat of his hands on my body, and I want more. Crave it in a way I've never craved anything except freedom.

"You said I could ask you anything," I say, peering up at him as we stroll deeper into the store, away from the prying eyes of the cashier. "Did you mean it?"

He glances down at me, amusement painted across his handsome face. "Lying to you isn't one of my sins, Brynna."

"Oh, sure," I mutter, rolling my eyes at him as I set my book back on the shelf. "He murders and maims, but he has a moral objection to lying."

"No." His lips twitch. "I'll murder, maim, and lie like a motherfucker if necessary. I said lying *to you* isn't one of my sins. I don't lie *to you*."

I reach out, tugging a random book from the shelf in front of us, processing. "Why not?"

"I want your trust," he murmurs. "You'll never give it to me if you doubt every word I say. You've been lied to so much in your life that trust is hard enough to come by without me getting in my own way here."

"How do you know I've been lied to?" I flip through random pages, not really paying attention, but trying to avoid meeting his gaze. Mostly because he's right, and I'm not entirely sure how I feel about it. The fact that he knows me so well is...unnerving.

"Because you still believe I'm the one who started this little war with your father." He sweeps strands of hair away from my neck, the brush of his knuckles against my skin sending a shiver through me.

"Did you?"

"No." His lips glide down the side of my throat, and I nearly drop my book. "He did, *mi cielito*. He's been putting his nose in my business, taking what doesn't belong to him."

"So you decided to take me," I whisper, my voice shaking.

"That was the plan until I met you." He curves his hand around my jaw, turning my face toward his. "It changed right here in this bookstore the first day we met."

"Why?" The question shakes on my lips, but I'm desperate to know the answer. And oddly...grateful that he's answering me at all. My father and Niall never do; he's right about that. Even when it's my safety at risk, they tell me as little as possible.

I'm supposed to remain loyal to a family and a business I know next to nothing about. And I get that they think they're protecting me by not exposing me to the things they do in the dark. But all they really accomplish by keeping me ignorant is...keeping me ignorant.

"Do you want the truth or a comforting lie?"

"I always want the truth, Naz."

"Because I wanted that fucking smile for myself, Brynna," he breathes, his lips inches from mine. "I wanted to know what it tasted like. I wanted to know what those pretty lips felt like wrapped around my cock. I wanted your light for myself." His lips brush mine as he nudges me deeper against the stack, pinning me between it and his hard body. His erection digs into my ass, and I bite my tongue, fighting a moan. "I wanted to break you and put you back together again, *princesa*."

I whimper this time, my core clenching as a wave of heat rolls through me. What would it feel like to be broken by this man? To be ruined by him? I ache to find out in a way I've never ached for anything.

"For the record, I still want all of those things," he whispers, running his lips down the side of my throat. "The things I want to do to you right here, right now..." He presses his open mouth to my skin, groaning. "*Fuck*, Brynna. You have no idea."

I think I do. I want the same thing with a desperation that's terrifying. But...I need to know something first. Something real.

"Who are you, Naz?" I whisper, hating the plea in my voice as I turn in his arms, meeting his gaze. But dammit, it is a plea. He seems to know everything about me, and I know nothing about him. Some terrifying part of me wants to trust him. And yet...who am I trusting? The enemy my father hates? The potently sexual man who says he wants to break me and put me back together again? The enigmatic man I've seen only glimpses of here and there?

If I'm going to take a flying leap, I need something real, something tangible. The wild hammering of my heart, the fire in my veins...that's only enough in fairytales. And this isn't a fairytale. In those, everyone lives happily ever after, and only the villain dies. But in this world? Well, he's the villain, and falling for him may kill us all.

And I'm dangerously close to falling.

Naz leans in close, his lips brushing my cheek. "I'm the man who would lay waste to this whole fucking city for you, *mi cielito*. I'm exactly who they say I am." His voice is a deep rumble against my skin, setting fire to entire tracts of my soul. "People call me the god of war. Do you know why?"

I shake my head, my knees trembling at the raw honesty in his amber gaze. It steals my breath, tangling me even tighter in his web.

"Ares was brutal in battle, but Scythians killed hundreds just to ensure he'd watch over their people because he was a protector, too. So am I." Naz pauses. "I am who I am because I know what it's like to lose everything to someone far more fucking vicious than me." A hint of pain flickers across his handsome face, a glimpse behind the ruthless mask. "I do what I have to do to ensure the man responsible doesn't take another goddamn thing from me or my people ever again."

My heart aches for the little boy who lost his family, who had his world ripped away before he was even old enough to comprehend what that meant for him. The scars his past left behind linger in his eyes now, the wounds still festering after all this time.

I realize in this moment that underneath the cold cruelty he wears like armor, he's deeply lonely. It's an ache I understand far too well. Even with Dad and Niall, this world is isolating as hell. I've always been alone in a crowd, separated by bulletproof glass and bodyguards. Unable to trust anyone because trust is deadly.

Naz and I are opposite sides of the same sad, lonely coin. He became a monster trying to keep his loneliness at bay, to live in this world without letting it destroy him entirely. And me? Well, I got trapped into being a good, obedient little princess.

His honesty about who he is and why is a stark contrast to my family's overprotective coddling. With my father and Niall, I'm a fragile little doll, safe but smothered. I'm supposed to be part of this world but untouched by it.

Will it be the same with him? With everything he's already lost, can he really give me the freedom I crave, or would giving into whatever is between us just be exchanging one pretty cage for another?

"Am I just another possession for you to protect?" The words taste bitter on my tongue, but I force them out anyway. I need to know. "Because I've spent far too long in one of those pretty prisons already, Nazario. My father promised my mom that he'd keep me safe, and he's never seen past that promise. He never will."

Naz slides his fingers into my hair, cradling my head, his expression soft. "Protection is a necessity in this world, Brynna. Your father understands that, just like I do. We guard what belongs to us because we know the agony of losing what we love. He's afraid of losing you."

My heart clenches at his statement. He offers my father understanding in a way my father would never return. In his shoes, my father would have sought to divide us, to sow doubt. But Naz doesn't try to turn me against him. He doesn't try to create a wedge between me and the man who raised me. He simply...defends him. It's a kindness I didn't expect from him, one that humanizes him in a way that nothing else could.

And it allows me to see him in a way nothing else has. He may be everything he said he was, but there's far more under those monstrous scales than I think anyone else will ever know. And those are the parts of him that fascinate me.

Maybe he is the god of war like people say, a brutal tactician who murders and maims as easily as he breathes. But he's all too human, too. And that part of him is just as fierce as the other parts. It knows kindness. It craves love.

Does he even realize that's what he wants? Perhaps not. Will he let himself feel it? I don't know. But the ability to feel it? That's there.

I rise up on my toes, pressing my lips. "Thank you," I whisper. "For being honest."

He groans against me, his arms tightening around my waist. "Brynna," he whispers, his hands fisting into my shirt. "*Dio, mi cielito*. You're killing me."

I think I'm killing me, too. I press my face against his throat, trying to get myself under control. Instead, I manage to knock the book I was thumbing through off the shelf.

Naz glances down at it and chuckles, unwinding himself from around me. His gaze flicks to mine, his amber eyes full of mischief as he bends to pick it up. "Is there something in particular in here that caught your eye, Brynna?" His deep voice sends a shiver racing down my spine. "Because I'm more than willing to put you in any position you point out, little one."

"What?" My brows furrow in confusion. Right up until I glance down at the book and realize he's holding a copy of the Kama Sutra, anyway. Mortification floods through me, heat blazing in my cheeks.

"Oh my God. I didn't...I don't..." I stutter, my tongue suddenly tied in knots. "This is so embarrassing."

"Embarrassing? No, *mi cielito*. You in any of these positions is a fucking dream come true." He flips through a few pages, his expression heated.

"You aren't helping," I groan.

He steps closer, crowding me up against the shelf again. "I'm not trying to help, Brynna. I like you trembling and sweet," he murmurs, his lips brushing the shell of my ear. "I like the flush to your cheeks and the way your pulse flutters." He nips my ear, his warm breath against my skin, stealing mine. "I like you thinking about me inside you."

I whimper, my knees quaking beneath me.

"Tell me, what filthy desires hide behind those innocent eyes, hmm? What is it that makes that sweet little body ache and burn?" he rasps, his voice gritty as he pulls back to look at me.

I swallow hard, my body trembling under his intense scrutiny. No one has ever looked at me the way he does—like he wants to consume me, possess me, worship me. Like he wants to own every thought in my head, every secret fantasy. It's thrilling and terrifying at the same time.

He trails his fingers along my wrist, branding me as his with nothing but his touch. "Do you want me to show you what you need so badly, Brynna?" he asks, his voice a seductive purr. "Do you want me to shatter you right here with entire worlds stretching out around us?"

Yes, I want to scream. I want it with an intensity that's terrifying. But the word lodges in my throat, trapped by the magnitude of this decision. If I give in now, let him in like this, there won't be any going back.

Naz will own me, body and soul. And I'll have willingly signed the deed.

As if sensing how badly I want to say yes, he lifts my chin with gentle fingers, forcing me to meet his gaze. "Let go, *cariño*," he croons. "Trust me with your body, even if you can't trust me with your heart. Let me give this to you. Let me worship."

The last of my resistance crumbles, swept away by the tsunami of desire his plea sends crashing over me.

"Yes," I breathe, that single word sealing my fate. "Show me what I'm missing, Naz."

A slow, wicked smile curves his lips. He leans down, his mouth a breath from mine as he presses the book back into my hands. "Flip through your naughty little book, Brynna," he murmurs. "Find a position that makes your cunt ache for my touch."

My hands tremble as I slowly turn the pages, each new explicit image sending a jolt of lust straight to my core. His fingers dance down my spine in a teasing caress that has me arching into him, silently begging for more.

He chuckles, the wicked sound pulsing against my clit. "So responsive," he breathes, slipping his hand beneath the hem of my shirt. The feel of his palm against my bare skin is electric. "I've barely touched you, and you're already quivering so sweetly for me."

I gasp as he grazes the underside of my breast, my nipples tightening into aching points. He traces the lacy edge of my bra, his touch maddeningly light.

I'm on fire, every nerve ending screaming.

"Please," I whimper, letting the book fall from my hands as I press myself up against him, desperate to feel him everywhere.

He hauls me up against his chest, the hard ridge of his erection pressing against my stomach. I rock my hips against him, the move instinctive, automatic. I want him to burn like I do.

He groans, his careful control splintering. "Careful, little one," he warns, his voice rough and gritty. "Keep teasing me, and I won't be able to stop myself from fucking you right here against the bookshelves while the cashier listens to you scream."

A wild thrill rushes through me at his words, the threat in them only fueling the ache consuming me. I want him to lose control, to claim me as if he can't stop himself.

I don't want calm, careful Naz, the man trying to prove himself worthy of me. I want the wicked prince who pillages and conquers and takes no prisoners. That's who he really is. Infinitely capable of love, kind when it matters, but ruthless and completely at ease in his own skin, with his own dark desires.

I meet his gaze, a challenge in mine. "Then do it, Naz," I dare him breathlessly. "Take what you want."

A muscle ticks in his jaw, molten hunger burning in his eyes. His hand delves into my hair, gripping the fiery strands as he tilts my head back. "Last chance to run, *cariño*," he rumbles. "Because once I have you, I won't let you go."

I fist my hands in his shirt, anchoring myself to his hard body. "I'm not running," I whisper. "I'm exactly where I want to be."

Something fierce and wild flares in his eyes, sparking a fire inside me as his mouth crashes down on mine. He steals the breath from my lungs, snatching it as if it belongs to him, as if I do. He doesn't kiss me, he claims my mouth, branding me as his.

I fall into it willingly, pouring everything I have into branding him back. I want him wrecked, too, shattered into pieces that I get to put back together.

His hand slides down my back to grip my ass, hauling me up until my legs wrap around his waist. The ridge of his cock nestles against my pussy, and I moan into his mouth, grinding against him shamelessly.

He tears his mouth from mine with a muttered curse. "Fuck, Brynna. Do you feel what you do to me?" He punctuates the question with a slow, deliberate rock of his hips. "Do you feel how fucking hard I am for you?"

Pleasure crashes through me in dizzying waves. I do feel it. God, I feel him trembling against me, so turned on his entire body shakes with need. My head falls back on a moan. "Naz, please..."

He captures my lips again, swallowing my cry of anticipation as he slips a hand between our bodies. His fingers graze my inner thigh, trailing higher, teasing my slit through the damp lace of my panties.

I jerk against him, a strangled moan tearing from my throat. I've never been this turned on, this desperate. It's like he's awakened something wild inside me, something not afraid to take what she wants, even in a fucking bookstore.

His fingers slip beneath the soaked lace, delving into the slick heat of my sex. I cry out, my nails digging into his shoulders.

"Oh, *princesa*," he breathes, his gaze flicking to mine. "No one has ever touched you before, have they?"

I shake my head, drowning in sensation as he plays with me, teasing me as if he knows exactly how to touch me, exactly how to break me.

"Good girl," he rasps, his eyes blazing with triumph. "Saving yourself for me. You knew I'd fucking kill anyone who had ever touched you, didn't you?"

"I..." I whimper, writhing against him. "God, please, Naz."

Two fingers tease my entrance, running in maddening circles before slipping inside. I gasp at the sudden intrusion, my inner muscles clenching around him.

"That's it, *mi alma*," he growls, his breath hot against my ear. "Fuck my fingers. Let me feel how tight this sweet little cunt is."

I moan helplessly as he pumps them in and out, stretching me, filling me. It's not enough, not nearly enough, but it's so damn good.

Electric pleasure radiates through me with each thrust. My head falls back against the shelf as I arch into him, my mind numb with pleasure.

"More," I beg shamelessly. "I need more, Naz."

"Greedy girl." His wicked chuckle has my thighs trembling around his waist. "Can you take one more, *princesa*?"

"I...I..." I whimper, hesitating. Can I? Should I? I don't know, but my inner muscles clench around him at the thought.

"Pull my cock out, Brynna. I want you to see what I'm going to ruin you with, little one. You'll beg for one more when you see it."

My hands shake as I fumble around, trying to obey. I finally manage to undo his belt, tugging at the button and zipper of his expensive pants with a desperation I've never felt before. I need to see him, to feel him.

I shove my hand inside, wrapping my fingers around his thick, hard length. He's so big, so fucking big.

God. How is he possibly going to fit inside me?

I glance up at him from beneath my lashes, a whimper lodged in my throat. "Naz..."

His amber eyes blaze as they meet mine. "Pull it out, *princesa*. Let me see those pretty eyes go wide when you realize exactly what I'm going to ruin you with."

I hold my breath as I pull him free, my eyes widening at the sight exactly like he said they would.

He's huge, long and thick, the broad head flushed a deep purple. A bead of moisture glistens at the tip, making me ache to run my tongue over it and taste him.

"One more, *mi alma*?" he rasps, his voice gritty. "Can this greedy little pussy take one more now?"

I nod frantically, beyond words, beyond thought. I just need him stretching me until I break apart in his arms.

Pride flares in his eyes as he adds a third finger, sinking them deep inside me. I cry out at the exquisite stretch, my back bowing off the shelf. The pleasure is edged with a sting of pain so sweet it's almost unbearable. I instantly love it.

God. What is he doing to me? What is he turning me into?

I moan brokenly as he fucks me with his fingers, stroking deep. Within seconds, I'm on the edge of something earth-shattering.

"Look at you," he breathes. "You're so fucking beautiful letting me wreck you. Do you feel it yet?"

"F-feel what?" I gasp, quivering on the edge of something so deep it's terrifying.

His lips slide along my cheek, seeking my ear. "You, handing your soul to the fucking devil," he breathes before nipping the shell of my ear.

The combination of his sharp bite and his words splinters me apart. I shatter with a cry, his name a broken prayer on my lips. And in that moment, I feel him slip into place in my soul, claiming a little corner of it as his own.

"Good girl, *mi alma*," he breathes against my skin, working me through every last aftershock. "Good girl."

"Naz," I whimper, pressing my face against his throat as my heart races and I gasp for breath. Bliss slides through my veins, turning me inside out.

Did I just hand the devil my soul? Probably.

Do I regret it? Not even a little bit.

"Brynna," he whispers back, nuzzling his face against me in a way that's achingly sweet. God, this man is nothing like I expected, and somehow, everything I expected at the same time.

The shrill ring of my phone shatters the moment before we can say anything else. I try to ignore it, desperate to cling to the blissful haze surrounding me, but it refuses to relent.

"Fuck," Naz mutters, lifting his head to look at me. Frustration burns in his gaze as if he knows exactly like I do that the ringing phone signals the end of our afternoon together. "You should probably get that, *mi cielito*."

I nod reluctantly, fumbling to pull the phone from my pocket. As soon as I see Niall's name flashing across the screen, dread washes through me. My last class isn't even over yet. He shouldn't be calling me for another hour. Whatever he wants probably isn't good.

"It's my brother," I whisper, my heart sinking.

Naz nods, his jaw tight. Understanding flickers in his eyes even as his lips compress into a thin line. He gently slips his fingers from my body, setting me on my feet.

I take a breath, already missing his heat, and then swipe to answer the call, my hand trembling as I put the phone to my ear. "Niall? Why are you calling me in the middle of class? What's wrong?"

I watch as Naz tucks his still hard cock back into his pants, his eyes locked on my face.

"Where on campus are you?" Niall's voice is tense, strained. Something is wrong. "I'm on my way to get you."

"What? Why? I have another class."

"Sorry, baby sis. Not today, you don't. 'Da wants you home."

"But..."

"Where are you, Brynna?"

"Dodd Hall," I whisper, meeting Naz's gaze. "What's going on, Niall?"

"There's been a development with Naz," he says. "You don't need to worry about it. 'Da just wants you home until it blows over."

"Blows over?" I narrow my eyes, my heart pounding. "What are you talking about? What happened?"

"See you in ten," he says, hanging up on me.

I huff a breath, squeezing my eyes closed as frustration and confusion swirl through me, alongside a healthy dose of fear.

God, what did they do?

"What's wrong, *mi alma*?" Naz asks, reaching out to stroke my cheek.

"I..." I shake my head, my tongue cloven to the roof of my mouth. How am I supposed to answer him? What am I even supposed to say? Sorry, but I think my family just screwed you over again while you had your fingers buried inside me? But please, let's do it again soon?

Hopelessness surges through me as the reality of the situation sinks in. This is an impossible situation of my own making. No matter what I do, I'm betraying someone who matters to me.

I'm betraying my family by being here with Naz, by giving in to the magnetic pull between us. By letting him touch me, shatter me in ways no one else ever has. And I'm betraying Naz by walking away now, by leaving him in the dark about whatever Niall and my father have done this time.

I'm caught between two worlds, two loyalties, and I don't know what to do. How can I possibly choose? How can I turn my back on either one of them?

"Brynna," Naz murmurs, tipping my face up to his with his fingers beneath my chin. "Talk to me, *princesa*. Let me fix it."

"You can't," I choke, shaking my head miserably as tears well in my eyes. "I'm sorry, Naz. I have to go."

His gaze drifts over my face, seeking some explanation, some answer. But I don't have one. I'm stuck, unable to tell him the truth, but equally incapable of lying to him. If hell exists, I think this is it.

I'm walking a tightrope, caught between duty to my family and desire for this complicated man. And I can't help but wonder if I'm strong enough to keep my balance...or if I'm destined to fall. If we're all destined to fall.

Naz's expression softens as he steps closer, leaning down to brush his lips across my forehead. "Go, *cariño*, do what you must. But this thing between us doesn't end here, not even close."

I'm not sure if he'll still mean that tomorrow, but I allow myself to lean into him for a moment, breathing him in.

"Be safe," I whisper. It's the only warning I can give him. I don't know if it's enough, but it has to be.

Please, let it be enough.

"Sweet, sweet Brynna," he whispers, his lips brushing my forehead again.

I wrench myself from his arms, my bottom lip quivering. And then I turn and hurry out before I lose the will to do it all.

CHAPTER SEVEN

Naz

"*Príncipe.*" Nicolas meets me at the elevator as soon as I step off, his expression grim. "We need to talk."

"Can it wait?" I growl, already striding toward my office. "I've got something to take care of this morning."

All I've been able to think about since Brynna ran off yesterday was the guilty, ashamed look on her face. It's driving me up the goddamn wall. I need to see her again, if only to reassure myself that the feeling of dread clawing through my fucking veins is my own imagination.

I don't know what her brother said to her, but it took every ounce of control I possess not to hunt the bastard down and put my fist through his face last night. She was right there with me, in my arms, her walls crumbling.

With one phone call, he sent them flying back into place. And I'm not entirely sure I'll be able to tumble them again this time. That's how shaken she was by whatever he said.

I know it wasn't just the call that rattled her. It was the fact that he called while I still had my fingers buried in her tight little body. She was still dripping around me, that perfect pussy gripping me like it never wanted to let go. Her sweet little pleas still rang around the shop.

He snatched away what should have been a moment of bliss for her and turned it into one of regret. I want to kill him for that.

But I fucking can't. Because if I do, I lose her for good. The little prick deserves to suffer, but if I make him pay, the only one I really hurt is the one least deserving of the pain. It's a moral quandary to end all moral quandaries.

Because I can almost fucking guarantee the prick is up to something. I knew it as soon as I saw her face. She may have been born in this world the same as I was, but she didn't come equipped for war. Her eyes don't lie. They're expressive windows right to her innocent little soul. And whatever her brother told her had to do with me.

Be safe.

Was she trying to warn me? Telling me the only way she knows how that her fucking family is up to something?

"It can't wait, Nazario."

I pause midstep, glancing over at Nicolas. His lips are compressed in a thin line, his jaw clenched with anger.

Dread washes through me.

"What happened?"

He cuts his eyes at the employees milling at the end of the hall, secretaries and whoever the fuck else works in this building, people we employ because running an empire requires more than cocaine. "We should talk in your office."

Whatever the fuck he has to say is bound to piss me off if he wants privacy to deliver the news. Fucking wonderful.

I jerk my chin in a nod, storming that way.

Thirty seconds later, I shove my way through the door into my office, Nicolas on my heels. The door slams shut behind him as I stalk to my desk. I don't sit. I'm too keyed up, too on edge.

If Nolan snatched another fucking business out from underneath me...

I need to move, or I'm going to fucking explode.

I wheel around to face Nicolas. "What the fuck is the problem this time?"

"The shipment that was supposed to arrive this morning never made it," he says, his tone clipped. He meets my gaze, unflinching, one of few men capable of doing it. Most are too goddamn afraid it'll end with a bullet between their eyes. Not Nicolas. He fears nothing.

"What did you just say?" I ask, my voice deadly calm.

"The shipment from San Diego never made it. We lost everything." He pauses. "Including Javier and Anton."

"Goddammit!" I roar, slamming my fist into the wall as rage courses through me in a roiling black cloud. Pain radiates up my arm from my split knuckles, but I welcome it, embracing the way it fucking burns as I shake off the drops of blood.

That stupid fucking prick. Does he have any idea what he's done? Anton has a fucking daughter at home, a little girl barely old enough to walk on her own. And Javier has a mother who relies on him.

"That shipment was over two million dollars, Nicolas," I say instead of saying any of that. What purpose would it serve? Nicolas knew them better than I.

"I know, Naz," he says, striding forward to grab the first aid kit from my desk drawer. He works silently, pouring alcohol over my bleeding knuckles and then dabbing it away. The cuts aren't deep, but they burn like a motherfucker.

"The fucking cops?" I growl when he's finished, but even as I ask the question, I know the answer. It wasn't the fucking Feds who killed my men and seized my drugs. The guilty, ashamed look on Brynna's face, her conversation with her brother...well, it doesn't take a goddamn rocket scientist to put the pieces together.

I put my hands on Nolan's pretty little daughter at the gala. I challenged him in front of everyone in that fucking room. And he swiped my goddamn shipment and killed my men to remind me that he bites back.

"No, it wasn't *los pitufos*." Nicolas stares at me levelly. "I believe it was Sullivan."

As if there was any doubt.

I close my eyes, fighting the rising tide of red-hot rage threatening to swallow me. He just killed my men and stole two million dollars worth of product from me. Two. Million. Dollars.

I grip the edge of my desk until the wood creaks beneath my fingers. I welcome the pain that shoots through my still-bleeding knuckles, embracing it, letting it ground me.

I can't fucking lose control. But *Cristo*, do I want to. That bastard just declared open war. If he wants a fight, I'll bring him a motherfucking reckoning.

But even as I think it, all I see is Brynna's face, her pretty eyes full of regret. The quiver of her bottom lip as she hurried away. The way she clung to me as if she didn't want to go. Her plea for me to be safe.

Fuck.

She's trapped in the middle, caught between me and her family. And I'm the motherfucker who put her there. No matter what happens from here, she's the one who gets hurt. And that's exactly what I swore wouldn't happen.

"What do you want to do, *príncipe*?" Nicolas asks.

Rain hellfire down on Sullivan until he's choking on the ashes of everything he's ever fucking built. But I don't say that. I fucking can't.

"How the fuck did they get their hands on my shipment, Nicolas?" I growl instead. "Who the fuck fed them the information?"

Nicolas hesitates. "I'm still looking into it."

"You don't know."

"No."

"That's a fucking problem, Nicolas. This wouldn't have happened if you'd found the motherfucking rat already," I snap, my voice ice-cold. "Bring me the goddamn list I asked for yesterday. I'll handle the problem myself."

"By gutting your own organization?"

"If that's what it takes."

"There are hundreds of people in this organization." He meets my gaze, his level. "Most do not know the Nazario I know."

"Meaning what?"

"You are not an easy man to work for," he says. "You ask me to find a needle in a stack of potential needles, and I look. But it's still a stack of needles. There is no loyalty because they don't know you. They fear you. Fear isn't enough."

"Jesus Christ," I mutter, scowling at him. "Not this shit again."

He shrugs. "I only tell you what you know is true. You need more than fear to lead. I know you. I know what you're capable of. They don't because all you give them is the same as you give the rest of the world. You bend for no one."

I tip my head back, cursing up at the ceiling. Maybe he's right, but I don't need them to love me. I need them to follow fucking orders. Following orders is what keeps them alive. It keeps Rojas off our doorstep. It keeps their families safe. Anything beyond that is a moot point.

"I'm not trying to be the goddamn King of England here, Nicolas. I'm trying to win a fucking war. No one has to be here if they don't want to be," I remind him. "They chose to follow. I expect loyalty."

"Yes, they follow because they believe you are capable of bringing Rojas down." He pauses, hesitating as if he isn't sure he should say what's on his mind.

"Just say it," I snap.

"They know what Rojas is. They've seen what he's capable of. They thought you were a better choice. But if all you offer is more of the same, can you blame them if they begin to wonder if there is a difference between you after all?"

"Enough," I snap, glowering at him. "That's enough, Nicolas."

He holds up his hands in a gesture of surrender. "I mean only to say...they doubt you because they don't understand you, Nazario. They fear you. And people who fear do desperate things. Picking out which is desperate enough to go to Sullivan is not easy."

Cristo. Is he right? Have I become so fucking consumed with winning this war with Rojas that I'm slowly morphing into some sick simile of the bastard? I've been fighting it for so fucking long I don't remember a time we weren't at war. And when I'm not at war with him, motherfuckers like Sullivan or Lombardi are in my face, rattling their swords against the front gate.

I told Brynna that I was a protector, that I do what I do to protect my people from Rojas. But did I lose the fucking plot somewhere? All I've ever wanted was to ensure that bastard doesn't take another goddamn thing, that he doesn't gain another inch of ground. What people think never fucking mattered. Keeping my boot on his neck did.

But if the cost is everything, I've failed. And at this point, if I'm poisoning my own people against me...maybe the cost is too high. Maybe I am failing.

"I'll find your rat, *príncipe*," Nicolas says after a moment. "We'll deal with him the way we deal with all rats. But chopping your nose to spite your face won't solve the problem."

I grit my teeth, nodding. "Fine. But I want him found, Nicolas. Before he does any more damage."

"Understood." Nicolas turns to leave and then seems to think better of it, turning back to me. "How are you going to deal with this situation?"

That's the two-million-dollar question, isn't it? How the fuck am I going to deal with the fact that Sullivan just hijacked my shipment?

I hesitate, searching for a solution that doesn't put Brynna in the middle, one that causes her the least amount of pain possible.

"Perhaps you should move up your plans for the girl," Nicolas suggests. "Take her out now and remind Sullivan that every move he makes against you will only increase his pain."

I'm moving before the last words even leave his lips. My hands close around his throat as I shove him up against the wall, cold rage a familiar fucking friend. I don't see him. I see a red haze. It whispers at me to end his miserable life right here, right now.

"*Príncipe*," he rasps, surprise flickering in his eyes.

"Suggest killing her again, and it'll be the last thing you do, Nicolas," I snarl, my voice like ice.

His eyes widen, his mouth going slack with shock. "Nazario," he says, and I read the truth in his eyes. He knows she isn't just a pawn.

Fuck.

I shove him away from me, breathing hard.

For a long moment, Nicolas doesn't say anything. And then he clears his throat. "My apologies, *príncipe*," he says softly. "I didn't mean to offend. I meant only to offer a solution. I didn't realize you were..."

He doesn't finish that sentence, but he doesn't have to finish it. I'm so twisted up over her that I'm attacking my own people now. *Dio*. What the fuck is happening to me?

Ha. Do I even need to ask?

I stride to the far side of the room, staring out at the city. Traffic is at a standstill, crawling at a snail's pace everywhere I look.

Dios de la Guerra, the god of war, the fucking cocaine kingpin, brought to his knees by a fiery Irish princess with sugar in her soul.

And despite it, I'm now forced to do something guaranteed to make things even more fucking complicated between us. Because if I let her father's attack go unpunished, every vulture in the city will be circling, looking for weak spots. And so will Rojas.

I can't allow that.

I'm on my knees for her, but I will never bow for that motherfucker. And I won't allow anyone else to bow before him either.

Sullivan has no fucking idea what he's done. To punish me, he may have just destroyed his daughter. And I'm the goddamn monster who started that ball rolling. I turned her into a pawn even after I swore I wouldn't.

Fuck.

Forgive me, mi alma. Cristo. *Forgive me.*

I shut off my emotions, locking them away in the black void of my soul where even I can't reach them, and then I turn to Nicolas and give my order.

"Find Josef, Andrés, and Griffin," I say, my voice cold and flat. "We have a message to send."

Nicolas nods, approval glinting in the depths of his eyes. "Where are we delivering this message, *príncipe*?"

"Sullivan's precious club," I say without hesitation. "I'm going to burn it to ash."

CHAPTER EIGHT

Brynna

By night, my father's club is a den of iniquity. Champagne flows, poured from the hands of waitstaff who make more here than they do modeling. The dance floor is packed with people willing to pay his price just for a chance to walk through the doors. Thousands of lights glitter and glint, turning it into a place outside itself, one where you can get lost for a few hours.

But by day, it's a sad reminder of the sins people visit upon themselves in the name of hedonistic delight. A fine layer of grim coats the floor, so trampled into it that there is no getting it out again no matter how hard the staff scrubs. The expensive dance floor has scuffs in it. The lights are dim, barely even lighting up the place. And the only thing you're liable to lose here is your sanity.

I should know. I've been stuck here since Niall shook me awake before dawn, telling me we needed to go. He wouldn't tell me why, but he didn't need to tell me.

They always move me out of the house when they've done something particularly dangerous. And since Nazario is their target this time...well, I'm pretty good at math.

Guilt is eating me alive. I should have told him...something...yesterday. Anything. I don't know what, but anything was better than nothing. *Be safe*. Does he know that I tried to warn him? Will he hate me when he finds out whatever my father and brother have done?

My soul trembles with anxiety at the possibility. It trembles with fear at the thought of what trespasses they may have committed against him.

Niall wouldn't tell me, of course. I tried to get it out of him, but he was as infuriatingly tight-lipped as ever.

I pace the edges of the dance floor, anxiety. Frustrated. Ready to snap.

My bodyguards clearly don't feel the same way. They're gathered around a table in the center of the room, knocking back a bottle of Jameson while they play cards. My father would probably lose his mind if he knew they were drinking on the job, but they always do when we're here.

The alternative is twiddling their thumbs, waiting for precisely what usually happens. Nothing. I may be a target, but the club is untouchable, a pillar in Beverly Hills. When even the mayor holds events inside, not even my father's worst enemies dare to touch it.

But they aren't Naz. My father may think he can handle him, but I think all he's likely to do is wake a sleeping giant. Naz isn't Adrian Lombardi or Eamon Callahan. He's in a class of his own.

"Twenty-five, motherfuckers." Cathán slams his hand down on the table behind me as he declares victory, making me jump.

"Son of a bitch," Conri growls. "How the fuck do you keep beating us?"

"Probably because hasn't drunk half a bottle. He can still fuckin' count," Seán mutters, earning a round of laughter from the other three.

I roll my eyes, turning back to the dance floor. I make another circuit, letting their laughter and joking wash over me, trying to focus on anything other than my own furious thoughts. Halfway through another circuit, something bangs against the doors to the club.

I turn in that direction, my brows furrowed in confusion. Is Niall back already?

Confusion turns to horror as the doors burst inward, splintering into pieces as if someone blasted them apart at the seams.

"Fuckin' hell!" Seán roars as four men storm into the club, guns drawn.

But it's not the four with guns I notice. It's the gorgeous devil behind them who captures my attention. *Naz.*

He strides into the club as if he owns it, cool self-possession in every step. He doesn't care that he shouldn't be here. He doesn't care that he's breaking and entering. He doesn't care about anything. His expression is ice cold, completely devoid of emotion as he steps over the threshold.

And then he sees me.

His amber eyes lock on my face, his expression morphing from ice cold to burning hot in a split second. It scalds me, stoking to life an answering blaze deep in my soul.

I take a step toward him, pulled like a magnet again.

And then something...flickers...on his face. Fear slides through his eyes, so much of it that it steals my breath. It's the first time I've seen that emotion from him. Perhaps the first time he's let himself feel it.

The sharp crack of gunfire explodes around me, bullets shattering glass and splintering wood. Splinters rain down around me as I drop to the floor, screaming.

"Brynna!" Naz roars, terror in his deep voice.

Terror surges through my veins, too, my heart pounding against my ribcage. I curl into a ball, covering my head with my arms.

Please, God. Please.

I'm not sure what I'm praying for. My safety? His? Theirs?

I sob as shot after shot rings out, along with grunts and curses. I don't dare lift my head, though. I'm too fucking afraid to look, to see. If Naz...

My mind catches on the thought, refusing to even form it.

The gunfire ends as abruptly as it started, fading to an eerie almost-silence. All I hear is my own panicked breathing, my own racing heart.

And then someone drops to their knees beside me, reaching out for me.

I cower away, sobbing. Screaming.

"Brynna, *mi alma*," Naz whispers. "I'm here. You're safe."

His deep voice cuts through panic, searing through the shards of ice around my heart. I sob his name, scrambling toward him.

He hauls me into his arms, holding me so tight I'm not sure which of us is more afraid in this moment, which of us is more grateful.

"Naz," I sob, burying my face in his throat, breathing him in. I let the scent of his expensive cologne wash through me, let the strength of his embrace root me to reality. This is the moment I exist in, not the terrifying few that just passed.

Footsteps thump across the dance floor, moving toward us. I shrink in his arms like a coward, trying to hide in his embrace.

"I've got you, *mi cielito*," he whispers against my ear, stroking his hand through my hair. "Nothing is going to happen to you." He lifts his head, his voice turning hard. "Everyone, get the fuck out. Now."

"*Príncipe*, what about...?"

"Get the fuck out, Nicolas," Naz growls, a ferocious warning full of menace and venom. I shiver at the sound, at the inherent authority in it. This isn't a request, it's a command to obey or suffer for it.

His man knows it, too.

"Everyone, out!" Nicolas shouts. "The *príncipe* says we're done here."

No one says a word as they retreat, obeying without question or complaint. Within seconds, the club is completely silent. Naz and I are the only ones left. At least, I think we're the only ones left alive.

I lift my head, needing to confirm my suspicions, but Naz stops me. "Don't look, *mi alma*," he murmurs, regret heavy in his voice. "There's nothing here you need to see."

And I guess that tells me everything I need to know. The men who were laughing only fifteen minutes ago, the ones my father sent to keep me safe, are dead. And the one he sought to protect me from now has his arms around me, comforting me.

Naz runs his hands all across me, his touch gentle. "Are you hurt, little one? Please, tell me you aren't." The pure agony, the fear, in his plea breaks my heart even as it heals some piece of it this day shattered. He meant it when he said he'd destroy this city to keep me safe. But an injury sustained because of something he set in motion? He'd destroy himself for that.

"I'm f-fine," I whisper, awed at just how deeply he cares. I'm the daughter of his enemy, the one who just did God knows what to him. And still, my safety is all he's thinking about, all he wants.

Does he realize that he's in love with me? Does he know that's what's happening to him yet? Why isn't he fighting it, railing and raging against it?

"I'm going to get you out of here," he murmurs, running his lips across my crown. "Keep your head down and don't look."

I should tell him no. That's the safe, sane thing to do. After what just happened—after whatever my father did—there's no escaping the fact that they're at war. If I leave with him now, it'll only fan the flames, incite more violence. But...I don't care anymore.

Naz chose his side. Now, it's my turn.

"I want to go with you," I whisper.

He rises to his feet with me tucked safely in his arms and carries me out of the club...and out of my cage.

He takes me to a safe house deep in his territory. It's a small little fortress, guarded by gates and wire. He sets me on my feet once we're over the threshold, only long enough to bolt the door and arm the alarm system.

As soon as both are done, I'm in his arms again. It's as if he can't stand the way they ache without me between them. He hasn't stopped touching me once since we left the club, hasn't stopped holding me.

He carries me past the living area toward a short hall, his lips against my ear. "I'm going to get you cleaned up."

I nod, more than willing to let him wash the stains of the last hour from my body. Like the rest of the house, the bedroom is small, cozy. Intimate. Dark, tasteful furniture rests on plush rugs. There is no artwork, no personal touches.

This isn't a home. It's simply a hideout, somewhere people stay when they need guns and razor-wire between them and their enemies.

He settles me on the edge of the bed, tipping my head back. His amber eyes bore into mine for a long moment, his fingertips gentle against my cheek.

"I'll be right back."

I bite my lip and then nod bravely, watching as he strides toward the bathroom attached to the bedroom. A few seconds later, I hear the water turn on. The sound is soothing, washing away the memory of gunfire and the grunts of my bodyguards as they fell.

It cuts off after a moment. Naz appears in the doorway with a washcloth in hand, his eyes immediately seeking mine as he strides toward me again.

We don't speak as he runs the warm cloth over my face, cleaning away the evidence of my tears. He's so gentle.

"What did they do to you, Naz?"

"Hijacked one of my shipments." A muscle in his jaw ticks. "Killed two of my men."

My heart trembles, guilt flowing through me in a giant black cloud. "I'm so sorry," I whisper, a fresh wave of tears already spilling over. "I..."

He immediately drops to his knees in front of me, setting the washcloth aside. His hands find my cheeks, capturing my tears. "You have nothing to apologize for, *mi cielito.*"

Nothing to apologize for?

"My father just took your drugs and killed two of your people, Naz."

"And I just killed four of his. We're even."

I hardly doubt they're even. I may not know much about drugs, but I'm guessing whatever my father stole was worth a small fortune.

"Is that why you were at the club?" I ask, trying to understand his logic. Why he's so calm about this. "To...kill my bodyguards?"

"No." His gaze flickers from mine and then back. "I didn't know you were there until..." He shakes his head, muttering a curse. But his hand shakes as if just the memory of seeing me standing there upsets him. "I was there to burn the place to the ground, Brynna."

"Oh." I probably shouldn't ask, but I do anyway. I have to know, to understand him. "Why didn't you?"

"You mean you don't already know?" He meets my gaze, his burning with that same intensity that overwhelms and excites and ignites me at once. The one that tells me whatever is between us has the potential to wreck lives or forge destinies.

"I..." I trail off, unsure how to answer. Do I know? I think so. I feel hope fluttering in my bones. But I need him to set it free. It can't fly until he does.

He leans toward me, eyes locked with mine, one hand against my cheek. His thumb sweeps along my bottom lip. "War doesn't matter. You do, Brynna," he says. "You've been in the middle your entire fucking life. I won't be the reason you're caught in the middle of this, too. I promised you that wouldn't be a pawn. I won't be the predator making you one now. You're safe with me. You'll always be safe with me, little one."

I sob his name, throwing myself into his arms as hope explodes through me, firing like a ball from a cannon. It ignites every inch of me, setting me ablaze.

He was right the day we met when he said that, one day soon, I'd want him to claim every piece of me more than I want air. That day is today. It's right now.

"Make me yours," I plead, digging my nails into his broad shoulders. "Please, Naz. Break me. Unmake me. I need it."

"Fuck," he growls, dragging me into his arms as his lips come down on mine. His kiss consumes me, branding me in ways his hands can't. He demands my surrender, and I give it willingly, my fingers tangling in the inky black strands of his hair.

His hands slip beneath my shirt, his knuckles raking up my sides as he slips it up my body. Our mouths part only long enough for him to slip it off over my head, and then we come together again, desperate, aching. Cool air kisses my skin as he reaches for my bra, nimble fingers tearing through the hooks.

The straps slip from my shoulders, leaving me bare to him from the waist up. He pulls back just enough to rake his molten gaze over me. Possession fires in his eyes as he reaches out, brushing his thumb across my right nipple.

"Oh, *mi alma*," he rasps, a thread in his voice that makes my core clench. "You're beautiful. But you're going to be fucking ravishing when these are covered in little marks to remind you that you belong to me now."

"Do it," I whimper, wanting to see it. Wanting proof on my body that he was here. That I'm his, and he's mine. I want evidence of his possession painted across my skin, screaming our defiance to the world. "Mark me, Naz. Claim me."

Pride and possession flare in his eyes. He drags me up against his chest, his mouth finding my right nipple. He sucks it between his lips, his tongue laving the peak.

I cry out, arching into him as pleasure spirals through me in a dizzying cloud.

His teeth graze my skin before he bites down. Pain collides with intense, blistering pleasure, and I writhe, sobbing in ecstasy.

His hands sink into my hips, holding me still as he switches to my left breast. Every touch of his lips against my skin is like a brand, claiming me as his. And every dark bruise he leaves behind sends another wave of need crashing through me.

"Naz," I whimper.

He seems to know exactly what I need more than I do.

"I've got you, little one. Patience."

But I'm not patient. I'm on fire, burning with need. Burning for him.

He hooks his fingers into the waistband of my leggings, dragging them down my hips and thighs, leaving me bare and aching. Possession and hunger smolder in the amber depths of his eyes as they rake over me, searing my skin, sparking an inferno inside me.

"So goddamn beautiful," he murmurs, his fervent praise leaving me trembling. No one has ever seen me naked before. I'm not a small girl. I never have been. I've got stretch-marks and rolls, dimples and imperfections everywhere. But the way he looks at me with so much desire, as if I'm a work of art, is a powerful, heady thing.

He rises, towering above me, tall and imposing. So fucking beautiful. With a smirk, he presses a hand against my shoulder, sending me sprawling across the bed.

"Watch me, *mi cielito*," he commands. "Don't take those pretty little eyes off me. I want you to see exactly what you've done to me, exactly how fucking hard that sweet body makes me."

My breath trembles on my lips as I nod, my eyes locked on him as his hands go to the buttons of his shirt. One by one, he slips them free.

I press my thighs together as he reveals perfect brown skin, inch by gorgeous inch. Tattoos swirl across his skin in intricate designs that whisper of pain and heritage, of honor and obligation, of secrets and the man behind the mask he wears like adamantine armor.

The shirt falls away, and my gaze drifts lower, over his rock-hard abs to the massive bulge straining against his slacks. I lick my lips, the ache between my thighs almost overwhelming. I want to know what it feels like to be owned by him, consumed, stretched and filled so completely I feel like it'll break me.

"Spread your legs, little one," he rasps, reaching for his zipper. "Let me see that pretty cunt."

My cheeks flush, but I don't look away from him as I slowly let my legs fall open, giving him what he wants. The intensity in his amber eyes as they home in on my sex is...God, I've never seen anything sexier than this man staring at my pussy like I'm offering salvation between my legs.

He undoes his pants, his eyes never leaving my sex as he shoves them down his hips. His massive cock springs free, long and thick, the head glistening with precum.

My core clenches, wetness pooling between my thighs as he wraps his fist around his shaft, stroking slowly from base to tip.

"Such a beautiful little cunt for a perfect Irish *princesa*, Brynna," he rasps, his voice a low rumble that vibrates through me. "I can't wait to see it stretched around my cock, your sweet virgin blood staining my skin as I fuck the innocence out of you." He squeezes his cock hard, stroking, tugging. "I intend to claim every last piece of it as mine."

His filthy words should frighten me...but they don't. I whimper, the ache between my thighs almost unbearable. I've never wanted anything more than I want him buried inside me, breaking me open and reshaping my shattered pieces into something new.

"Please," I breathe, spreading my legs even wider in a blatant, eager invitation. My hand slips down my stomach, sliding across my pussy. "Do it, Naz. Take it. Destroy me."

He snaps, roaring like a wounded beast as he falls on me, ravenous, pushed to the edge of his control. His hand lashes around my ankle, yanking me to the end of the bed.

I cry out in bliss, in surrender, as he drops to his knees between my legs, the look of abject worship, of utter devotion, on his face searing.

He buries his face between my thighs, his beard scraping against my skin as he devours me, his hands rough, his tongue hot.

I cry out, my back arching off the bed as he seals his lips around my clit and sucks hard. Explosions of ecstasy rip through my body.

"Such a sweet little cunt, *mi cielito*," he growls, backing off to run his tongue in maddening circles around my hole. "I could lick it all day." He pries my cheeks apart, his hands so damn rough and perfect, his gaze burning as he stares at my exposed back entrance. "And this tight little asshole... *Fuck*, I can't wait to claim it, too, Brynna. Want to feel it strangling my cock as I force myself inside. You'll love every filthy second, *princesa*."

I whimper, my cheeks burning at his wicked promise even as it sends another flood of wetness trickling between my thighs. No one has ever spoken to me the way he does, so raw and wanton. So hungry for me. He doesn't ask nicely or guard his tongue. He isn't a polite gentleman, afraid to cross my father. He tells me exactly what he wants, exactly what he's going to do to me. And I fucking love it.

I want it, every filthy word, every depraved desire. I want this man broken open, spilling every bit of his darkness into me. I don't want to be a perfect, pampered little princess. I want to be *his*.

He licks over my asshole, and I sob, writhing against his face. "Please, Naz..."

"Please what, *mi alma*?" He nips my inner thigh before flicking his tongue against my asshole again. "Tell me what you need. Beg for it, and I'll give it to you. Whatever you want."

"I need your tongue inside me. I-I need you to fuck me with it," I plead shamelessly, too far gone to care about what I'm allowed to say or should want or what's proper. Here, none of that matters. With him, there are no rules. There's just give and take. There's pillage and conquer and fuck and claim.

"That's it," he rasps, his voice an approving rumble that sets me on fire. "Beg for my tongue in this tight little asshole like a good little slut."

"Please, Naz," I sob, writhing beneath him, desperate for more. "I need it. I need you. Lick me open and fuck me apart."

He groans his approval, nipping my inner thigh. "Whatever you want, I'll give you, Brynna. Down to my fucking soul."

His tongue laves over my asshole in long, slow strokes that make me shake and whimper. Each touch is a tease, a torment, and a revelation all rolled into one. And I'm burning alive, my skin on fire, my blood molten lava roaring through my veins in pyroclastic flows.

"More," I plead, fisting my hands in his hair. "I need more."

He groans against my skin, the tip of his tongue pushing against the tight ring of muscle. It resists the intrusion for a long moment, fighting against him, refusing to let him in. But Naz refuses to be denied...and so do I.

His tongue slips inside, claiming. Conquering.

The sharp sting gives way to blistering pleasure.

I sob in ecstasy, mindless, boneless. His in a way that shouldn't feel this fucking good.

I chant his name, sobbing it like it's the only damn thing I know.

He spears his tongue into my asshole, forcing it deeper, fighting for every atom of space he claims as he fucks me with it. Possesses me. Unmakes and breaks me.

He groans against me, and the vibration of sound resonates through my body, amplifying the explosions already ripping me apart at the seams.

I shatter, falling into a million jagged pieces. Gushing all over his face as tidal waves of ecstasy crash over me.

In a split second, I'm flat on my back on the bed, pinned beneath his weight. Every inch of him seams to me, holding me down, and I fucking love the way it feels to be this consumed by him, to be held down by him, completely at his mercy.

He pants above me, his amber eyes on fire as he stares down at me, an inferno raging in his eyes. "Fucking perfect," he rasps, pressing a sweet kiss to the corner of my lips. "God, *mi alma*. You're perfect."

I tremble at his praise...and then tremble again when he wraps a firm hand around my throat, squeezing just enough to make me gasp.

My eyes fly to his as he yanks my leg up over his hip, opening me up to him. His cock slips through my folds, grinding against my clit before he notches himself at my entrance.

"Are you ready to break for me, *princesa*?"

"Yes," I gasp, arching, straining toward him, desperate and eager.

I expect him to be rough, to take me hard and fast, to pound into me until I shatter. To fuck me with the same ruthless intensity he does everything else. But Naz is many things. Cruel to me isn't one of them.

When he presses forward, he's gentle. Reverent.

His eyes bore into mine as he pins me down and stretches me open slowly, carefully. Even then, the sheer size of him burns. I gasp, my nails scoring into his broad back, my teeth sinking into his shoulder. But the pain is sweet, fleeting. One I don't want to end.

"Breathe, little one," he croons, his lips against my skin. "Just breathe through it. I've got you."

I inhale a shaking breath as he continues to press forward, inch by torturous inch. When he's finally buried to the hilt, splitting me open at the seams, he goes completely still, giving me time to adjust.

His eyes meet mine, molten and hungry. But there's no mistaking the soft reverence there, either. The complete adoration.

"You feel like heaven," he rasps, brushing his lips against mine. "So fucking tight and perfect around my cock."

"Naz," I whimper, tears stinging the corners of my eyes. He's breaking me, but not in the way I expected. This side of him, this sweetness...God, he's perfect in a way that hurts.

"Are you ready for more, little one? Ready for me to fucking destroy you?"

"Yes," I gasp, quivering on the edge of something vast, something so powerful it's terrifying. It feels like forever. But what do I know about forever? What does that even look like in our world? He may have made a different choice today, but we're still predator and pawn. I'm still who I am...and he's still who he is.

But even so, I think it looks like this. It looks like him.

"Good." His lips skim along my cheek, seeking my ear. His breath blows hot against the shell of it. "Then let me hear that pretty voice, Brynna. I want you to fucking scream while I fuck my way into your soul. It belongs to me."

Oh, God... No, not God. *Nazario.*

His eyes meet mine as he withdraws almost all the way and then slams back inside me, bottoming out. I scream just like he wanted as ecstasy pours through my veins, igniting in a liquid rush.

"Fuck," he groans, intense pleasure flaring in his eyes. "Scream like that again, Brynna."

His hips snap against mine a second time, the force of it shaking the bed beneath us. I throw my head back, shouting his name as another wave of ecstasy pours through me.

"That's it," he whispers. "Just like that, *princesa*. Let the whole fucking world hear you falling apart on my cock."

I sob his name, clawing down his back deep enough to draw blood as I cling to him, completely at his mercy. Except...he has none as he fucks me so hard and deep stars burst behind my eyelids.

I shouldn't love it. Ecstasy shouldn't rip through me with every ruthless thrust. And yet, I do. It does. This is what's between us, what's been roiling beneath the surface since I dropped my books at his feet. This is my darkness, my sin. It's him and the pure fucking pleasure of being owned by him, dominated by him...turned inside out and upside down by him.

I'm not my father or my brother, lulled by money and power or the thrill of being a criminal. I'm enthralled by this—by the complete loss of inhibition. It's like stepping outside myself, giving in to all those temptations I've always judged myself for. But there are no judgments here. There's only *yes* and *more*. There's something so simple, so pure in the freedom of it, and it's fucking beautiful.

His hand tightens around my throat, and I clamp down around him, my walls fluttering and clenching.

"Fuck," he groans, his cock twitching inside me. "Your sweet little cunt gets so fucking tight when I choke you." He squeezes harder, and spots dance in my vision. But my walls clamp around him again because he's right. I do love it. "Such a filthy little *princesa*. I knew you'd love all the dirty things I want to do to this body."

He kisses me hard, his tongue delving into my mouth. He fucks me with it in the same brutal way his cock pounds into me. I whimper against his lips, trembling as my orgasm builds, cresting higher with each snap of his hips against mine, with each tiny sliver of air he allows me to take.

There's something almost feral in his amber gaze, something beautifully unhinged and wildly, desperately, wholly *mine* as he stares down at me. I think he's more himself with his hand around my throat and his cock inside me than he's ever been.

Naz has found where he belongs. He's found his purpose. It's me. It's this. And fucking hell, it's beautiful, twisted devotion.

"I'm going to fucking ruin you, Brynna. Break you open and pour myself inside you. When I'm done, you'll be my perfect little Irish fuck doll, unable to breathe without me."

"Yes," I gasp, the edges of my vision going hazy as I hurtle closer to the edge. "Do it, Naz. I need it. Need you so fucking bad." I want him in my skin, painted inside my veins like a tattoo.

He snarls, and then his hand is gone from my throat. Before I can protest the loss or appreciate the rush of air, he flips me onto my stomach. His cock never even leaves my body.

He drapes himself over me, his chest against my back as he slides a hand into my hair. I cry out as he forces my head back, baring my throat to him.

"Your body is mine now," he rasps, against my ear, rolling his hips. His cock drags along my walls, hitting something deep inside me that makes me quiver and wail. "Your pleasure belongs to me."

"Yes, yes," I chant, unable to deny it.

His hand tightens in my hair as his other arm bands around my waist, hauling my hips up to meet his thrusts. He pounds into me again and again, wrecking and ruining me, leaving me shattered and scattered and so damn high on him, nothing else matters..

His teeth scrape the side of my throat before settling against my ear. "This is what we are together, *mi luz, mi alma, mi amor*," he breathes, panting for breath as he drives into me again and then again. "This is who we are."

He's right. We aren't predator and pawn, destined for destruction. We're something else...something far more profound. We're simply Naz and Brynna, irrevocably tied to one another despite my family or his organization. Despite our world. Despite everything.

We're as inevitable as the tide, as unavoidable as war.

I don't break. I surrender—to it, to him—and willingly hand over my soul.

He cranes my head back, forcing me to arch into him. I feel every ridge of his cock dragging along my walls, stretching me, reaching the deepest parts of me.

"Let go for me, *mi amor*," he rasps against the shell of my ear. "Fall apart on my cock like you were fucking born to do."

"Naz," I sob as he turns my face toward his. His mouth crashes against mine, his kiss consuming. I bow to him...fall to him. And shatter.

Ecstasy licks along my nerve endings, igniting me from the inside out. I whimper into his mouth as the waves slam into me, stealing sight and sound. Stealing here and now. Stealing everything but him and the hot pulse of his cum as he groans my name like a prayer…and falls to me, giving me everything he has.

All the way down to his beautiful, monstrous soul.

CHAPTER NINE

Brynna

"I don't want to go," I admit, my bottom lip quivering as Naz and I say goodbye a few blocks away from my father's house.

He reaches out, stroking the back of his hand down my jaw, his eyes soft. "I'll break you out without hesitation, little one. Just say the word."

I know he means it. If I call him for a rescue, he won't even hesitate to show up on my father's doorstep. He'll bring an army if that's what it takes. And he won't leave without me.

But...I don't want it to come to that. If there's a way out of this without more bloodshed, I want to find it. Despite their flaws, despite everything, I love my father and Niall, and I know they love me in the same fierce way. They aren't bad men. They're simply men, just like Naz. They're flawed and complicated and frustrating as hell. But they're my men, my family.

If there's a way out of this...well, there has to be a way out of this.

"Just let me try," I whisper. It's all I can do. Try. Go reassure my father and brother that I'm alive and try to keep them from escalating this war any further.

Naz jerks his chin in a nod, his amber eyes glittering with repressed emotion. "Be careful, Brynna. If they try to keep you from me..."

"They won't," I hurry to say, my soul quivering. "I'll stick to the story. It'll be fine." I place my hand on his arm, trying to calm him. "Just let me try, Naz. Please."

He exhales a sharp breath and then nods again, his thumb against my bottom lip. "Do what you must, *mi amor*. I made my promise already. I won't break it."

I practically fling myself across the console against his chest, pressing my lips to his. He consumes me with his kiss again, searing his brand onto my soul, into my lungs. I accept it willingly, eagerly, breathing my own back into him.

And just like yesterday, I wrench myself out of his arms before I lose the willpower to do it at all. I throw myself from his SUV and slam the door, my feet flying down the sidewalk as I race toward my father's house, tears in my eyes.

If this doesn't work, I'm going to lose someone else I love. Cancer already stole my mother. Will war still Niall? My father? Naz? Am I going to be the reason the people I love destroy each other?

No. I'll wage war myself before I let that happen. I've gone along with their plans and been their obedient little princess my entire life. I haven't made waves. I've stayed in my place. I've done everything I was supposed to do because they said I was supposed to do it. Because I loved them enough to do it.

I've enabled them to my own damn detriment. I'm not doing it anymore. I know who I am now and what I want. His marks are still painted across my skin. His possession still sings in my veins.

He may be the god of war, but I'm the one who drove him to his knees. I'm not weak. I'm not helpless. I'm *his*.

"What the fuck are you doing?"

I wheel around, yelping as Niall's furious voice rips through the shadows half a block from the house.

He steps out from behind a tree, his furious green eyes locked on my face as he stomps toward me, dressed in the same suit he left in this morning. Only it's wrinkled now, and he looks like he's been through hell today.

Crap. He and my father have probably been worried for hours.

"You scared the crap out of me, Niall," I say, guilt whispering through me. It seems like every damn decision I make lately causes harm to someone I care about.

Naz swept into my life, turned it upside down, and everything has been spiraling out of control since. It would be easy to lay the blame at his feet, but it isn't his fault.

It's Newton's Third freaking Law. We're two objects colliding into one another, one no more responsible for the force of impact than the other. But the force of the collision bound us together, and the energy rippled outward, impacting everyone and everything around us.

"What the fuck were you doing with him?" Niall growls, his voice level.

"I..." I lick my lips, anxiety shooting through me.

"We've been tearing this fucking city apart, worried out of our goddamn minds that he was holding you hostage after he killed your bodyguards," he growls. "And he just brings you home?"

"I can explain," I whisper.

"Really?" His upper lip curls. "You can explain the fact that you threw yourself into his fucking arms and kissed him, Brynna?"

Shit. He saw us.

I didn't anticipate that, didn't plan for that. I didn't mean to kiss Naz this close to my father's house at all, honestly. But I did it anyway. Because when it comes to him, I can't stop myself.

"What the fuck are you thinking?" Niall asks, shoving a hand through his tousled hair. His voice is rough, the betrayal in it cutting bone deep. "It's Nazario fucking Leyva."

"Don't," I whisper.

"Don't what? Remind you who you're dealing with?" He shakes his head at me, clearly frustrated. "He's dangerous, Brynna."

"You mean like you and Dad? Because people say the same thing about the two of you, Niall," I remind him, crossing my arms to glare at him. I don't know if there's a chill in the air or if it's in me, but I feel cold all the way to my bones. "He just doesn't pretend he's someone other than who he is the way you and Dad do."

Niall's lips compress into a disapproving line, but he doesn't say anything. He can't because he knows he's wrong here. Judging Naz for doing the same things he and Dad do every day is the height of hypocrisy.

It's sad, really. Niall wants to look down his nose at Naz and treat him as if he's somehow beneath him because of who he is, but they're cut from the same cloth. Naz is just more honest about who he is than my brother has ever been. He wants the mobster life and the reputation, but not the stains that come with it.

He can't have both. It doesn't matter how hard you scrub; blood doesn't come out once it's stained your soul. Naz understands this. My brother has yet to learn that lesson.

"He killed your bodyguards, Brynna," Niall says, his voice softer. "Men you've known for years. You know we can't let that stand."

"And why do you think that happened, big brother?" I ask, staring him right in the face. "What do you think could have possibly driven him to that point?"

Niall clenches his jaw, his gaze shifting from mine.

"You and Dad have been attacking his organization for months. You've snatched businesses out from beneath him just to keep him from getting them. You've taunted him, pushed him, and what has he done in response, Niall? Until you killed two of his men and stole his drugs, what was his big crime?" I demand. "He talked with me at a freaking gala! That's it."

"He's using you," my brother grits out. "How do you not see that, Brynna? You've been down this road before. Our enemies think they can push you around on the board like a goddamn chess piece to get to us. Cavallari did it. Callahan tried it. Gregori, Peterson, Alamanti... Do you really think Nazario fucking Leyva is any different?"

"You don't even know him."

"And neither do you," he snaps, fire in his eyes. "All you know is the lie he's sold you. Whatever you think this is, it ends now."

I gape at him. "You don't get to tell me what to do, Niall. This is my life. Why can't you just let me live it for once? Why do you want me miserable so damn badly?"

He stares at me for a long, silent moment before he shakes his head. Something almost...sad...floats through his gaze. "I've never wanted you miserable, *deirfiúr*. I've only ever wanted you happy and safe. Everything I've ever done, I've done to protect you."

"Yeah, well, maybe I'm tired of being a perfect little princess in a glass cage," I whisper, my throat burning as tears prick at my eyes. "Maybe I've been tired of being her for a long time, Niall."

He swallows, his jaw pulsing with emotion. "End it with Nazario, or I'll tell 'Da," he says. "You know what he'll do if he finds out that he put his hands on you."

I stumble back a step, shock coursing through me. "You wouldn't."

"That's where you're wrong, baby sister. I would. I will." He holds my gaze, and I see the truth glittering in the depths of his eyes. Even if I hate him for it, he'll do it. Because I may chafe against my bonds...but he never has. He's my father's obedient little prince. And if I was born to be free, he was born to follow.

"Do it, and I'll never speak to you again, Niall. Neither of you," I whisper, my voice shaking with emotion. My hands shake, too, fury and devastation coursing through me. My own damn brother would betray me, pit the man I love against the man who raised me. All because duty matters more to him.

Surprise flares in his eyes, as if I've startled him this time. "You'd choose him over your own family?"

Would I? Can I? Is that really the choice I'm going to be forced to make?

"Yes," I say, meeting his gaze, unflinching. "I'd choose him, Niall. Today or any other damn day, I'd choose him because he already chose me."

"Jesus Christ," Niall mutters, his lips twisting. "If you believe that, you're more naïve than I thought, Brynna."

"He wasn't at the club today because of me, Niall. He intended to burn it down because of what you did." I pause a moment, letting that sink in. Without the club or the books my father keeps hidden inside, we'd lose millions. Potentially enough to ruin this family. "He changed his mind because he chose me instead. So yeah, I'd choose him. He deserves for someone to put him before this stupid war." I shoot my brother a sad smile. "And so do I."

I don't wait around for a response. There isn't anything else to say anyway. I turn and head for the house, leaving Niall to make up his own damn mind. He will, anyway.

Half an hour later, my father is still hugging me when Niall stomps inside.

"Look who is home safe," Dad says, relief coloring his tone. "Your sister is a clever girl, Niall. She ran out the back and hid until she thought it was safe to make her way back here."

As far as stories go, it's paper thin. But my father has always preferred to believe a comforting lie than a hard truth when it comes to me. It's his weakness. He doesn't want to see what's right in front of his face, so he doesn't let himself.

Niall flicks his gaze in our direction and grunts. "Welcome back. I'm going to shower. I've got some prick's blood all over me."

I didn't see it outside, but he's right. Flecks of it stain his pants. It crusts his cuticles.

My heart clenches.

"What did you do?" I whisper.

He meets my gaze, his burning. "What I had to do. Thought you were being held hostage by a monster."

"I wasn't," I say, iron in my voice.

"Yeah, well, it's not like I knew that when I was trying to beat answers out of the motherfucker's man," he mutters.

"Niall!" Dad snaps. "Enough. You don't talk to her like that. She isn't part of this."

Niall glances from me to him. "Maybe it's time she is, 'Da. She's old enough. Might as well let her know what this family is willing to do to protect its own."

"I don't need to know," I whisper, my voice shaking. I've got enough guilt seared into my conscience. I don't need more.

"Yeah, you do."

God. Why is he doing this? To prove a point? To punish me?

"Go on," he says. "Tell her what you plan to do to Nazario for what he did today. She should hear it. How else is she supposed to protect herself?"

Dad hesitates, and then his eyes narrow. "I'm going to destroy his organization from the inside out using his own man against him."

I blink, my blood running cold. "What man?"

My dad smiles, a cold, vicious smile that sends a shiver ripping down my spine as he pats me on the head. "You don't need to worry about that, *iníon*. Just keep yourself far away from Nazario Leyva, and let us worry about the details."

Niall meets my gaze, something glinting in his eyes that I don't understand. "Yes, keep yourself far away from Nazario," he says in a flat, emotionless voice that sends a chill racing through me. "Even his own people see him for the soulless monster he is. You don't want to end up caught in his trap."

He turns and walks away without another word, leaving me trembling in his wake. I know he was just trying to get a rise out of me...but the fact that one of Naz's own people is helping my family is terrifying.

Is Naz in danger? Am I?

Ha. Is that even a question? There's been nothing but danger since I dropped my books at his feet. And if there's danger now, it changes nothing.

Do his people really see him as a soulless monster?

A protest wells up from the depths of my soul at the thought. Naz is many things—dangerous, ruthless, brutal, a criminal, and a killer. Maybe he's even a monster. But he isn't soulless. Not even close.

CHAPTER TEN

Naz

"You need to make a move against him, *príncipe*," Nicolas argues. "If you don't, he will only grow bolder."

"Enough," I growl, throwing up my hand as my patience with him runs out. He's been hounding me about this for two goddamn days now. Ever since I informed him that Niall Sullivan had killed another of our men.

Brynna cried when she delivered that news in a hushed whisper over the phone the night I dropped her off at home. I'm mad as hell I couldn't pull her onto my lap and console her. I'm furious she feels guilt at all. This is not her fight; it's not her war. And yet, she feels obligated to try to end it anyway.

I don't know what the fuck Niall did with Josef's body, but we've yet to find it. That point isn't sitting well with Nicolas. He wants to strike.

But I can't. So long as Brynna is determined to stay in that house and try to end this peacefully, I won't risk her. With one of my own goddamn men aligned against me, I can't. It's too dangerous. I trust that her father won't hurt her. But a rat? Someone willing to betray his oaths? There's no telling what he's capable of doing.

But the moment she calls me and tells me she's done? The instant she's safely behind my walls? I'll do what the fuck I need to do. She won't be in the middle then. She'll be mine, under my protection. Safe. And I'll make damn sure everyone knows that I'll take any move against me as a direct threat to her.

They'll either heed my warning or suffer the consequences. A reckless, savage part of me hopes whoever the fuck is working against me is foolish enough to tempt fate. Part of me hopes her father is, too.

Because of him, she's there instead of in my arms, in my bed. I haven't had my hands on her gorgeous body, my fucking tongue on her tasty little asshole, my cock in her perfect cunt, in two days.

I'm not a happy man.

"But *príncipe*..."

I slam my hand down on the desk, rattling a paperweight off the side. "I said enough!" I snap. "I'll make a move when

I'm good and goddamn ready. Until then, shut the fuck up, and get back to work figuring out who the fuck is trying to rip this organization apart!"

Nicolas falls silent, frustration burning in his gaze as he stares at me. For a long moment, he says nothing. And then he mutters a curse. "Love has blinded you, Nazario."

"What did you say?" I snarl, gripping the edges of the desk to keep from launching myself across it.

"I'm sorry, *príncipe*," he says softly. "But the men are starting to talk. They think you've grown weak, that you're betraying your oaths and your people. Your organization is under attack, and you hesitate. Your people die, and you do nothing." Nicolas shakes his head, disappointment heavy in his gaze. "This isn't you."

"Get the fuck out," I say, my voice deathly calm.

"I'll go," he murmurs, holding up his hands. "But I'm merely the messenger. I want what's best for you. You know this."

"I said get the fuck out, Nicolas."

He sighs heavily, striding for the door.

As soon as it closes behind him, I grab the stapler, whipping it across the room. It slams into the wall, ripping a hole through the plaster.

The destruction that rains down doesn't calm the rage pulsing through my veins.

He's wrong, goddamn him. Brynna isn't the source of my weakness. She isn't the reason I hesitate. Whoever the fuck is stabbing me in the back is the one who has me all fucked up in the head. They're the reason I question my decisions, doubt what the fuck I'm doing.

They're a goddamn cancerous rot, infecting everything. They're feeding information to Sullivan, trying to dismantle my entire empire from the inside out. Stealing from me, from everyone.

A soft knock sounds against the door.

"Fuck off!" I roar.

Nicolas doesn't fuck off. The door clicks open...and Brynna steps through.

I'm on my feet, across the office to her in three strides.

"Brynna, *mi amor*," I breathe, dragging her into my arms before the door even clicks closed behind her. "What are you doing here?"

"I had to see you," she whispers, melting against me. "I missed you, Naz."

Dio. She's killing me.

"What about your father and brother?"

"They think I'm on campus. They won't come looking," she promises. "They're in some meeting." Her lips slide along the underside of my jaw. "I don't care if they do. I needed your arms around me."

I grip her hips, my cock throbbing at the little thread in her voice. She's horny, aching. *Cristo*. Brynna wants to come.

"That isn't all you need, is it, *mi cielito*?" I ask, tipping her head back to brush my lips against hers. "You came here for something more, didn't you?"

She whimpers against my lips.

"Answer me, little one."

"Yes. Please, Naz."

I press the tip of my thumb into her perfect mouth, groaning when she immediately wraps her lips around it, sucking instinctively. *Fuck*. This perfect little *princesa* doesn't even know what she does to me. "Tell me what you want me to do to you, *mi cielito*."

Courage flares in her emerald eyes, darkening them. "Use me, Naz. Fuck me. Make me forget everything but you."

"How should I use you, hmm?" I press my thumb deeper into her mouth, fascinated by the way she sucks like an obedient little toy. "Should I choke you with my cock, Brynna? See how much you can fit down your pretty little throat?"

"Yes," she whimpers around my thumb.

"Maybe I should press you up against the windows and fuck you in front of the city, let everyone watch you beg me to defile and destroy you."

Shit. Maybe I'll do both, see how much she can take today. I'm in that kind of mood. It seems like maybe she is, too. She came here to fuck, to forget. And I'll be the goddamn master of her memories if that's what she wants.

My fingers tangle in her silky hair as I push firmly against her shoulder, guiding her to her knees. "Be a good girl and take my cock out," I command, my eyes locked on her perfect face. "Wrap those pretty lips around me and choke on it like the obedient little slut you are."

Her hands tremble as she reaches for my belt, fumbling with the buckle. A groan rumbles from my chest as she pulls my zipper down and slips her hand inside, freeing my aching cock.

"Fuck, *princesa*," I hiss as she wraps her hand around the base of my shaft, stroking me like she owns the goddamn thing.

Her tongue darts out, flicking her plump bottom lip like she can already taste me on it, and my cock jerks, precum beading at the tip.

She flicks her gaze up to mine, her emerald eyes dark with desire, silently begging for permission. As if I'm going to tell her no.

I fist my hand in her hair and guide her forward until her lips brush against my head. "Open," I rasp. "Take me deep, little one."

She eagerly parts her lips, enveloping the head of my cock in the hot, wet perfection of that mouth.

I groan, my knees shaking as she wraps her tongue around my crown, lapping at the cum leaking from my slit. *Dio*, she's good at this, a natural little cocksucker. Like she was made to be on her knees with my cock between her lips.

She bobs her head, lips stretched wide as she takes me deeper, her hand stroking what she can't fit.

"That's it, *mi amor*," I praise. "Just like that. Relax your throat for me. Let me fuck that pretty face."

She whimpers around me, the vibrations sending sparks of pleasure zinging through me. I curse under my breath and thrust my hips, pushing deeper.

She gags slightly but doesn't pull away.

"Fuck, such a good girl," I praise as I fuck her face with shallow thrusts, letting her get used to the sensation. "You love choking on my cock, don't you? Love the way I use your pretty mouth for my pleasure."

She moans her agreement, flattening her tongue along the underside of my shaft as I pump between her stretched lips, forcing my cock deeper.

Saliva drips down her chin, coating my balls.

I growl, fisting her hair with both hands now, holding her in place as I slam into her throat, my balls slapping against her chin with every thrust. She takes it like the perfect little cockslut she is, gagging and sputtering, tears leaking from her eyes, still looking at me with complete submission in her eyes.

I pull out, letting her gasp for air. She pants, lips swollen and slick with spit, pride blazing in her eyes.

This fucking *princesa...Dio*. I said I was going to break her. It was a motherfucking lie. She's already broken me, changed me, turned me from a goddamn monster to a desperate, deranged motherfucker willing to do anything just for a taste of her. Just for a smile. Just for the fucking honor of being the one who touches her like this, fucks her like this.

I'll raze this empire to the ground myself for this. For her. It'd be worth it. No question about it.

"Stand up and walk to the window," I command.

She shakily gets to her feet, stumbling to the floor-to-ceiling windows overlooking the city. I grab her hips and yank her back against me, grinding my cock against the curve of her ass.

"I'm going to fuck you right here against the glass," I breathe in her ear. "I'm going to pound this needy little cunt until you're screaming my name for all of LA to hear. You want that, *mi cielito*? You want everyone to know who this pussy belongs to?"

"Yes," she whimpers, pressing back against me.

Of course she does. Because this girl was made for me, desire for desire, sin for motherfucking sin.

I roughly tug her skirt up over her wide hips, yanking her lacy panties down her thighs. She gasps as I tear open her blouse, buttons pinging across the floor. I unhook her bra with a deft flick, freeing her perfect breasts.

"Hands on the glass," I order.

She obeys instantly, flattening her palms against the window like the greedy little thing she is.

I step back, drinking in the sight of her—naked except for her heels, splayed out for me, the city sprawling beyond. Fucking gorgeous.

I trail my fingers down her spine, over the swell of her ass. She shivers, goosebumps rising on her alabaster skin.

I groan when I slip my hand between her legs, my fingers sliding against her soaked thighs. I find her already dripping cunt. "Did choking on my cock get you this wet, *mi amor*?"

"No," she breathes, arching into my touch as I circle her swollen clit with my thumb.

"No?" I arch a brow.

"Your hands on my body did. The way you speak to me did. *You* did. Choking on your cock made me almost come. Please..."

Fuck. Her honesty is a treasure, something to protect at all costs.

I press two fingers into her tight cunt, and she cries out, clenching around me. I curl them, finding that sensitive spot inside her, and rub mercilessly.

She writhes against the glass, her full tits flattening obscenely on the window.

"Look at them down there," I murmur against her ear, pumping my fingers faster, harder. "Going about their lives, no idea that up here, an innocent little *princesa* is about to get fucked within an inch of her life by the big bad cartel boss they're all so afraid of."

"Naz!" she sobs, bucking against my hand.

I add a third finger, stretching her open. Fuck, she's close already, fluttering around me. Such a desperate little thing.

"Are you going to come on my fingers, *mi cielito*? Coat them in your sweet cream so I can lick them clean after I ruin you?"

"Yes! I'm...I'm..." Her orgasm crashes over her, and she wails my name, convulsing against the glass.

"Good girl, *princesa*. Come all over my hand," I croon, working her through it until she's plastered to the window, trembling and spent.

I don't give her a reprieve. I want her wrecked, demolished with pleasure. I line myself up with her entrance and slam in to the hilt with one brutal thrust.

"Fuck!" she screams, scrabbling at the window.

I grip her hips, my fingertips digging into her soft flesh to hold her in place as I fuck into her, taking her hard.

I reach up to palm her tits, plucking at her nipples, and she screams, throwing her head back against my shoulder.

I pinch her nipples harder, twisting the sensitive peaks until she's writhing against me, impaled on my cock. "That's it, *mi alma*. Take it. Take everything I give you like the greedy little slut you are."

"Oh god," she sobs, her pussy clenching around my shaft as I pound into her. "Naz, I can't...it's too much!"

"You can and you will," I growl. Releasing one of her tits, I reach down to press my fingers to her swollen clit, rubbing tight circles. "I know this greedy cunt needs more, Brynna. It's never satisfied, is it? Always hungry for my cock, my tongue, my fingers. Such a desperate little hole."

She whimpers, shaking her head frantically. We both know it's a lie.

I tug on her nipple in reprimand.

"Don't lie to me, little one. I feel you dripping all over me, soaking my cock and balls. Your pussy is begging to be used hard. It wants to be stretched and filled and fucked raw."

"Please." Her voice breaks on a sob, her hands scrabbling uselessly on the window, trying to find purchase, trying to find something to anchor her as I do exactly what she wanted me to do. Use her. Fuck her. "Please, Naz..."

"Please what? Use your words, pretty little *princesa*."

"Please let me come!" she wails, her pussy clenching hard around my cock. "I need it! I need you!"

"That's it, *mi cielito*," I rasp in her ear. "Beg for it. Beg for my cock like the desperate little slut you are."

"I'm begging!" she sobs. "Please, please, Naz! I'll do anything! Just let me come on your cock! *Please*!"

There's something so sweet about the way her voice breaks when she begs, about the way she whimpers and whines. About the way tears leak from the corners of her eyes. She's fucking beautiful when she's ruined, ravishing when she's this lost in pleasure. Nothing exists to her but me, her, and the intense need ripping through her veins.

She isn't a perfect little *princesa*, worried about war when she's on my cock, begging to come. She's just Brynna, wild, free, more fucking mine than anything has ever been before.

And goddamn, the way I love her is terrifying.

I latch onto her shoulder, biting down as I pound into her, my fingers flying over her clit. She detonates with a scream, her cunt clamping down on my cock, rippling and gushing all over me as she convulses in ecstasy.

"Fuck!" I roar, slamming into her one last time before I explode. I grind against her, emptying every last drop inside her as her pussy continues to ripple and massage my spurting cock.

She whimpers my name, the sweet sound squeezing my heart in a vise as she collapses into my arms. I wrap them around her, pulling her up against my chest, shaken to my core at the way I love this girl. At the things I'd do for her.

I scoop her into my arms, carrying her toward the sofa on the far side of my office. She burrows into me, her face pressed against my throat.

"Are you okay, *mi alma*?" I murmur, running my lips across her crown, my hands across her perfect body...bringing her back down as gently as I can.

"Yes." She groans, pulling back to look at me. Her glossy eyes shift across my face. "I think I should be asking you that, though."

My brows furrow.

"There's a hole in your wall and a stapler on the floor," she murmurs. "And you yelled for me to fuck off before I opened the door."

Shit. I didn't even realize she'd noticed the stapler.

"Difference of opinion with one of my men," I mutter.

"It required a stapler to go flying?"

"That was the result." I shrug.

"What happened, Naz?" She strokes my jaw, genuine concern in her emerald eyes. "Do you want to talk about it?"

Do I? Fuck no. Should I? Probably. Because even now, with her in my arms, fury still threatens to slide through my veins. The desire to rip this goddamn empire down around me is...powerful. I'd rather topple it myself than risk letting Rojas get his hands on it because some prick thinks he knows better than I do.

Loving her hasn't blinded me. The exact opposite is true. For the first time in my life, I think I'm seeing clearly. And the future I see? It's not more of this shit.

Heavy is the motherfucking head.

"Do you ever wish you were someone else, little one?" I ask wearily.

She laughs softly. "Only every day since I met you, Naz."

I tip her chin back, forcing her to look at me. "What does that mean?"

"I was just kidding."

"You weren't. Explain."

She bites her lip and shrugs, her gaze darting away from mine and then back. "I don't think I can stop this war," she whispers, her voice small in a way it's never been. "I keep looking for a way, keep hoping, but..." She exhales a shaking breath, her bottom lip quivering. "There isn't one. I'm going to lose my family, Naz. Or you. That's how this ends for me. So yeah, I wish I were someone else."

I cup her face in my hands, my heart aching at the pain in her voice. "Look at me, Brynna," I command softly. When she does, I see the tears shimmering on her lashes. "I won't let that happen, *mi amor*. I promise you."

"How?" she whispers. "How can you possibly promise that? This is so much bigger than us. It's your entire organization."

"Nothing is bigger than us." I brush the tears from her lashes. "*The whole world is divided for me into two parts: one is she, and there is all happiness, hope, light; the other is where she is not, and there is dejection and darkness*," I whisper, knowing instinctively that she'll recognize the line from *War and Peace*, that she'll understand.

"Naz," she breathes, her expression softening.

"You're what I need in this world, Brynna. More than this fucking empire. More than my own goddamn life. I'll tear it all down myself if that's what it takes to end it. I love you, little one."

Her breath catches. "W-what?"

"You heard me. The predator fell in love with his pawn." I brush my thumb over her plump bottom lip, smiling at the way her eyes widen. "*Te amo*. I love you. Nothing is bigger than that. Nothing matters more than that."

Tears spill down her cheeks as she launches herself at me, wrapping her body around me. "I love you too, Naz. So much that it terrifies me."

I crush her to my chest, burying my face in her fiery hair as my entire being shakes. *Cristo*, three little words. Three perfect little words. "I know, *mi amor*. I know."

She clings to me for a long moment, just letting me hold her, adore her, *love* her, before she pulls back, meeting my gaze.

"Why do you want to be someone else, Naz? There's nothing wrong with who you are." Her sweet smile is everything. It's redemption. It's salvation. It's peace.

"Perhaps not," I murmur. "But this goddamn empire has become a yoke around my neck."

"So cut it." She touches my cheek, her fingers gentle. "You make the rules. If these cause you pain, make new rules."

"Maybe you're right," I murmur, turning my face to kiss her fingers. Perhaps that's exactly what I need to do.

CHAPTER ELEVEN

Naz

Sullivan's club is already reopened for business, every trace of what happened here just a few days ago already wiped clean. No surprise. The incident didn't even make the news. I'm sure he greased the pockets of every politician and cop he knows to keep it under wraps.

It's what he does. It's who he is.

The oversized motherfucker working the front door doesn't try to stop me as I stride past him. Music pumps through the club, the beat vibrating my bones. Strobe lights spin and dance overhead, giving me a fucking headache.

I'm barely four steps in before I've got three of Sullivan's enforcers trailing me.

I ignore them, skirting around the dance floor toward Nolan's office in the back. He's expecting me. I made sure to give him that goddamn courtesy before I showed up. It wasn't out of respect but necessity. I don't want the prick putting a bullet in me before I say what I came to say.

I promised his daughter that she wouldn't lose me. If I have to haunt this bastard for proving me wrong, I'm going to be pissed about it.

I lift my hand to rap my fingers against his office door, only for one of Sullivan's men to step forward, his expression level as he clears his throat. "Everyone who goes in there gets patted down."

"Oh, for fuck's sake," I growl, rolling my eyes. Do they really expect me to take him out by my damn self in a club full of his people? Either they think I'm seriously the fucking devil...or an idiot. I turn, lifting the sides of my suit coat. "Do I look like I'm armed?"

"Have to check," he grunts, shrugging.

I bite my tongue, jerking my head for him to hurry it the fuck up. Naturally, he takes his sweet time, patting me down like he expects to find an entire arsenal hidden beneath my shirt.

I mutter a curse when his hand crawls all over my dick.

"That's my cock," I grit out.

He sweeps lower, grabbing another handful of it.

"Still my motherfucking cock," I snap, one brow arched. "Satisfied now, or do you want to grab the final four inches of it too?"

"Jesus Christ," he mutters, stepping back with a disgruntled look on his face. As if I had my hands all over his cock. "He's unarmed."

I shoot him a cold look, pinning the other two with it as well. They fidget under the weight of it, uncomfortable, unsettled.

Good. They should be.

"I'm not your fucking enemy," I growl before turning to rap on Sullivan's door. I don't bother to wait for an answer before I step inside his office, letting the door slam closed behind me.

His office is as predictable as the man himself. Expensive scotch bottles line shelves behind his imposing desk, the Irish flag stretched across one wall. Awards hang on the other three walls, mingling between photos of his family and those he's taken with celebrities and whoever the fuck else this man thinks will lend him a little legitimacy.

It's almost laughable how zealously he's curated that image. He's every bit as monstrous as I am, every bit the criminal. He loves the power. He loves the game. But he chases legitimacy like he thinks catching it, surrounding himself with it, will make him anything other than what he is.

He looks up at me, an infuriating mix of anger, curiosity, and cold amusement in eyes too goddamn much like his daughter's. The hint of triumph glinting in their depths, as if he thinks I'm here like some beaten dog, makes me homicidal.

Cristo. I want to flip that desk and wrap my hand around his throat, remind him exactly who the fuck I am. But I'm not here for that. I'm here for her. I'm here...to make new rules. To be something—to forge something—different.

I told her to choose peace the day we met, but it isn't hers to choose. It never was. If I want peace in her life, it's up to me and this motherfucker right here to choose it for her.

I'm willing to give her that. Is he?

"Leyva." He leans back in his leather chair, smirking. "Looking for something?"

My jaw clenches, anger coursing through me. The prick thinks I'm here to beg for Josef's body back. He's waving it in my face like a flag in front of a bull, hoping I charge at the bait.

"I'm not here for Josef's body, Sullivan. We both know you aren't giving it up so he can be buried," I mutter. "Decency is only in your nature when people like those in the photos on your walls are watching."

His smirk slips at the insult. "Then why are you here? I have a club to run."

"I'm here about your daughter."

Surprise flares in his eyes, followed by steely anger. He flattens his palms against the top of his desk, his body stiffening. "What the fuck do you want with my daughter, Nazario?"

"You already know, Sullivan. You knew the truth the minute she came back to you unharmed. You just didn't want to admit it."

"Say it, you fucking prick," he growls.

"What is it you want to hear? That I've been seeing her since the gala?" I ask, shoving my hands into my pockets to hide the way they shake. I've never been a man to show vulnerability, to lay my cards on the table for anyone to see. And baring my fucking soul to a man who'd use it against me in a heartbeat is the epitome of uncomfortable.

But when that man is Brynna's father? The one capable of helping me ensure she's safe? I'll slice my veins open and bleed if that's what I need to do.

"Do you need to hear that I'm in love with her? That she feels the same way?" I grit out. "What do you need to hear to end this fucking war for her sake, Sullivan? Tell me, and you'll hear it. Every goddamn word of it will be true, too."

His eyes widen before his face contorts with rage. He leaps to his feet, his chair crashing against the wall behind him. "You motherfucker! You've been manipulating her this entire time, trying to use her to destroy me."

"No, I haven't. I considered it. I wanted to make you squirm, take her from you, and break you, and then I met her." I hold his gaze, letting him read the truth in my eyes. "She isn't something to be used, Sullivan. She isn't a pawn. I haven't asked her a single thing about your family. I haven't tried to get a single scrap of information from her. The last place I want her is in the middle."

"You lying bastard," Nolan practically shouts. "You killed her fucking bodyguards!"

"I came to burn this club to the ground," I snap, and even though I shouldn't, I appreciate the little sliver of fear that flares in his eyes. It feeds my soul. "She's the reason it's still standing. As a matter of fact, she's the only reason I haven't ripped through your entire goddamn family like a missile. *I don't want her in the middle.*"

"If she's in the middle, it's because you put her there," he snarls, leaning over the desk, his eyes narrowing to icy slits. "You put your goddamn hands on her. On my daughter!"

"And you put her in a cage," I growl, my hands clenching into fists. "How much longer do you think she was going to survive it, Sullivan? How many more bodies do you think you could pile on her conscience before she snapped? One more? Two?"

"What the fuck are you talking about?"

"Open your eyes!" I roar. "Your daughter? The one you're so worried about now? She's been drowning in your care for years! But you were too busy looking the other way to even notice, so don't stand there now and act like I'm the monster for loving her. Someone needed to."

Maybe he loves his daughter, but he hasn't loved her right. He put her in a cage and neglected to notice that it wasn't nearly big enough for her. It was smothering her, killing her light. And he just let it happen, over and over again, day after fucking day.

Brynna wasn't meant for a cage. She wasn't meant to be smothered. She needs more than that. And this prick has had his head too far up his own ass to realize that his brand of protection was a death sentence for her.

"If you want to hate me for setting her free, so be it. I can't stop you. But she will be free. And she won't be in the middle of this war. I didn't come here to beg. I didn't come to plead. I won't get on my fucking knees, Sullivan," I say, my lip curling as I stare at him. "I came to give you a chance to do right by her because it's what she deserves. But I'll force you and your family with my boot on your neck if that's what I have to do to protect her."

Nolan slams his fist down on the desk, the crystal tumblers and decanter on top rattling violently. His eyes blaze with fury, a vein pulsing at his temple. "You think you can come in here and threaten me? Threaten my family? I will wipe you and your entire fucking empire from existence before you touch my daughter again, Leyva."

I laugh softly. He still doesn't get it. He still thinks this is a war. It isn't. The rules have changed. This is a hostile takeover. And I'm willing to swallow any poison pill necessary to do what needs to be done.

"You aren't hearing me, Sullivan. She's what matters. She's the *only* thing that matters. I'll rip it all apart if that's what it takes to protect her. Try to take her from me, and I'll burn your fucking world to the ground," I say, striding toward the door. "Insist on continuing your little war and I'll raze your empire and mine both. When I'm finished, there won't be anything but ash left."

I leave him standing there, spluttering and cursing my existence, as I step out into the hall, slamming the door behind me. He can try to fight me. He can try to continue this war. It'll only cost him everything in the end. The only things I'll leave are Brynna, Niall, and a fucking roof over the old bastard's head.

And I'll inflict the same damage on my own empire if that's what it takes. I'll raze it to the goddamn ground and start again.

Fuck Rojas. Fuck duty. Fuck everything.

I'm done.

I've been this man for long enough. My people want someone new? They're going to get him. But they really shouldn't have bit the hand that feeds them. Because new Nazario? He's done sacrificing everything for an empire he never wanted in the first place.

"Nazario." My name pulses over the music thrumming through the club.

I glance to the left, muttering a curse, when I see Niall step out of the shadows beside his father's office door.

Fucking great. Now I have to deal with the other one. And I like this one less than the one I just walked out on.

"What?" I snap, keeping my hands in my pockets...away from the temptation of his throat. I haven't forgotten the shit he said to Brynna at the gala. Nor have I forgotten that he's the one who snatched bliss from her at the bookstore.

Niall steps closer, his lips compressed into a thin line, his expression tight. And just like in that office, looking into his eyes is like looking into Brynna's. They're so much alike that it's eerie. Except there's no innocence here, and whatever light he has left is dim and dull, tarnished so badly it'll never truly shine again.

"We need to talk," he mutters, sounding exactly like a motherfucker who'd rather be saying anything else.

"So talk." What? I don't plan on making it easy for him. I've had my fill of bullshit for the day.

"I heard you in there," he says.

"If you're here to threaten me, get on with it. I've got shit to do."

His jaw tightens, a muscle ticking. "Don't be a fucking asshole, Nazario. I'm talking about what you said about Brynna."

"Ah. So, you're here to fight."

"No." He glares at me. "I'm asking if you meant it. Because the only thing in this world that matters to me is her. And that's the only reason I kept my fucking mouth shut about the two of you."

Well, fuck.

"I've done a lot of fucked up things in my life," I murmur, giving him the truest answer I know how to give. "But your sister?" I swallow hard. "She's the one thing I've gotten right. Yeah, I meant it. Every goddamn word."

Niall jerks his chin in a nod. "Then you should know that one of your men has been sending us information on your organization for the last year. They know everything about you and your business."

"I gathered as much when you hijacked my shipment," I mutter, not revealing the one and only piece of information about their family Brynna did reveal to me—my fucking rat.

"You don't know everything I do," he says, dragging a hand down his face. "Your man isn't your man, Leyva. He works for Rojas."

I freeze at the sound of Rojas' name falling from his lips. At confirmation of what I already suspected. The betrayal stings even though it shouldn't, even though I should have been prepared for it.

Cristo.

"Why are you telling me this, Niall?"

"Because my sister was at your office earlier today," he says, his eyes locked on me as if daring me to deny it. "And after the shit that just went down in there, I'm guessing she'll be spending a lot more time with you soon. Her safety has always been my priority, and if Rojas's man gets his hands on her, he'll kill her just to break you."

"Fuck," I mutter, my stomach twisting at the thought. But he's right. I've considered it myself. If Rojas has a man inside my organization, he wouldn't hesitate to kill Brynna just to destroy me. *Cristo.* He killed my entire family just to destroy my father. And he's been trying to kill me ever since. He doesn't like to lose, and to him, I'm a living, breathing reminder that he lost, that he failed. Until I'm dead or he is, he'll never forgive that.

"Maybe you were right in there and we fucked up, smothered her," Niall says. "I don't know. But you were right about her being miserable." He glances away as guilt flickers in his eyes. "She's been miserable for a long goddamn time."

At least he can admit it, even if their father can't. *Dio.* At least one of them knows her well enough to recognize it.

"As much as it pains me to admit it, Leyva," he continues, "she isn't miserable with you. You make her happy for some goddamn reason. So when she comes to you, I need you to fucking guarantee that you meant what you said in there, and you'll keep her safe, even if it means dismantling everything."

"This empire is your future." I motion around us. "You'd tear it down for your sister?"

He meets my gaze, the truth glittering in the depths of his eyes. Perhaps there's a little bit of light left in him after all. It's her. She's his light just like she's mine, idolized by the brother who helped raise her. "In a fucking heartbeat," he growls.

"Then you know exactly how far I'm willing to go to protect her," I murmur, meeting his gaze. "You have my word, Niall. I'll do whatever it takes to keep her safe."

He stares at me for a minute, searching for any hint that I'm playing him, that I'm a threat to his sister. But he finds none. There is none. So he nods reluctantly. "I'd really like to hate you," he mutters. "You just fucked everything in there."

I cock my head to the side, staring at him.

"You don't know, do you?" he asks, surprise filtering across his face.

"Know what?"

"She chose you, Leyva. As soon as he confronts her, she'll be on your doorstep," he mutters. "He won't give her a choice. Not after that."

"Fuck," I curse, my heart clenching. "That wasn't what I wanted. It isn't what she wants."

"Yeah, well, shit doesn't always work out that way." He places a hand on the handle of his father's door. "Take care of her."

I nod, watching as he slips inside his father's office. Fuck. I wanted her with me, but not like this. I may have solved one problem and created an entirely new problem.

I scrub a hand down my face, and then turn and make my way back out into the club. As soon as I step out of the hallway, the three fuckers from earlier are on my ass again.

They follow me all the way to the damn doors.

Because I am who the fuck I am, I flip them the bird as I sail through, stepping out into the night.

"Cocky prick," the one who patted me down mutters under his breath.

"You'd know. You had your hands all over it," I call over my shoulder, striding toward the SUV Nicolas has waiting on the curb.

I climb into the SUV and settle against the leather seat as Nicolas merges into traffic.

He glances over at me. "How did it go, *príncipe*?"

I stare at him for a long moment, searching his face, trying to read behind the familiar lines I've known for half my life. The man who's been my right hand since I was a teenager, who I thought I could trust with anything. But doubt niggles at the back of my mind now, refusing to quiet.

I sigh heavily, pinching the bridge of my nose. "Our rat works for Rojas," I mutter.

His eyes widen before he schools his expression. But I catch the flicker of unease, the tightening around his mouth. "Fuck. Do they know who it is?"

I shrug, looking out the window at the city blurring by the windows, neon signs and streetlights streaking in a kaleidoscope. "Probably."

I feel his gaze on me, probing, questioning. But I don't offer anything more. It's a shitty day when I trust Niall Sullivan more than my oldest friend. But here we are.

For the first time since I met him, I'm not sure where his loyalties truly lie. Oh, he's loyal to the Leyva name, I have no doubt. But is he loyal to me? Does he serve Nazario?

I've never had a reason to question it before. He's always been the devil on my shoulder, ready to whisper encouragement or condemnation in equal measure. He's seen me at my worst and never flinched.

But Brynna changed the game. She changed me in ways I didn't see coming. In ways Nicolas never anticipated. Falling for the enemy's daughter? Being willing to destroy everything to keep her safe? It goes against everything I've ever done. Everything I'm supposed to be.

This organization—this empire—is supposed to come before all things. Keeping Rojas at bay and protecting my people has always been the priority. No matter what I had to sacrifice. No matter how brutal, bloody, or violent I had to be.

The people still matter. Keeping Rojas at bay still matters. But Brynna? She's my soul.

Shit. Maybe the whispers were right, and I didn't have one. Not until now. Not until her.

So it begs the fucking question...where does Nicolas's allegiance lie now? Would he side with Rojas if he thought I was losing my grip on the throne?

I hate that I'm even thinking it. But in this world, doubt keeps you breathing. And trust gets you killed.

"Perhaps it is time to cull the ranks, Nazario," he finally says, glancing over at me again.

"Maybe it is, Nicolas," I murmur, closing my eyes. "Maybe it is."

CHAPTER TWELVE

Brynna

I'm prepared for my father's wrath before the front door ever flies open, slamming against the wall so hard family photos crash to the floor. Naz called to warn me what he was going to do. I didn't try to stop him.

Surprisingly, Niall called once it was done. I didn't expect that. Things between us have not been good the last few days. Actually, they've been awful. He hasn't spoken a single word to me. It's killing me, but if he hates me for telling him the truth, I can't change it.

The fact that he called gives me hope that maybe things aren't broken irreparably between us.

I've been waiting in the living room for my father since Niall's call, my hands folded together in my lap, my heart in my throat.

He's barely over the threshold when he notices me. As soon as his fiery gaze lands on me, he explodes. "Tell me he's a goddamn liar!" he roars, flecks of spit flying from the corner of his lip.

He's unhinged in a way I haven't seen since the day my mom died, like his world is ending. He tore the house apart in his grief and rage that day. God only knows what damage he did outside these four walls. Niall adamantly refused to talk about it when they stumbled in, covered in blood, at dawn, but I know it was bad.

We had peace for months. For the first time in my life.

My throat burns at the sight of him so close to that edge again now. Disappointing him was the last thing I wanted to do. But I'm tired of disappointing me, too. I'm sick of barring the doors to my own damn cage and pretending that's the way it has to be just to keep him and Niall happy.

"It's true," I whisper, my voice steady even though my heart feels like it's in a vise. "Everything Naz told you is true."

Dad storms across the living room toward me, his heavy steps thundering against the hardwood floor. He reaches me in four long strides, his hands clamping down on my shoulders, his fingers digging into my flesh. "How the fuck could you betray your own family like this? For him?"

I cry out, fear pulsing through me. For the first time in my life...I'm afraid of this man. "You're hurting me," I whisper, struggling against his hold.

He mutters a curse, releasing me as if my words scalded him. Regret flashes in his eyes as he stares down at me, a modicum of sanity dimming the red haze.

"Jesus Christ, Brynna." He runs a shaking hand through his silver hair. "What the fuck have you done?"

Tears burn the backs of my eyes, but I blink them back. I won't cry now. It's a weakness I can't afford. "We fell in love, Dad," I say softly. "If anyone can understand how that feels, I thought it would be you."

He loved my mom beyond reason. He lived for her, breathed for her. And losing her broke him. It's been years, and he still isn't over her. He never will be.

"If you believe that, you're a fucking fool," he spits, the words like venom on a tongue that's never said an unkind word to me before now. "The man is incapable of love. All you are to him is a pawn, a pretty little plaything to use."

"You don't know anything about him," I growl, anger welling up from my soul. He doesn't know what he's talking about. If anyone should be able to see beyond the surface, my father should. But he's so blinded by hatred that he refuses to even consider it. "He makes me happy. Happier than I've ever been."

"He's a fucking criminal, Brynna! His hands are so bloody, it's a wonder they aren't permanently stained red."

"You're one to talk," I snap, beyond tired of everyone judging Naz for the same damn sins they've committed. "Or have you forgotten about the empire you built on blood? I certainly haven't. I live with the memories haunting me, with the guilt and regret staining *my* soul."

"Everything I've done has been to protect this family! To protect you."

"Maybe that's what you tell yourself, but we both know you did it for power and pride," I say. "Everyone who targeted me, you killed because you could. Because they dared to insult you. It had nothing to do with me, Dad. It was all about you. And so long as you had your power and your pride, you didn't give a shit what it did to me."

Pain roils in his eyes, aging him. He seems...older, weathered in a way he never has before. There are cracks in his armor, chinks I've never noticed before now. "I've given you a good life, Brynna."

"No," I whisper, shaking my head. "You gave me a cage and called it a life, hoping I'd never realize the difference. You made me complicit in things I never wanted, never asked to be part of. It's different with Naz. I know exactly who he is and what he's capable of. But he gave me a choice, Dad. You never gave me that." I pause, tears blurring my vision. "He loves me. Why can't that be enough for you?"

"Because I don't want to bury my only daughter!" he roars, slamming his fist into the wall. The plaster cracks beneath the force of the blow. "One way or another, he'll get you killed. I won't stand back and watch it happen. You aren't seeing him again."

I thought my heart would crack in half when this moment came...but it doesn't. Too much of it belongs to Naz now, his name emblazoned and branded across entire tracts of it. Instead, a small corner of it crumbles, shattering into pieces.

"You're wrong," I whisper, reaching down to scoop up the bag I packed earlier. "I am seeing him again, Dad. I choose him."

He stumbles back a step, shock painted across his familiar face. "You don't mean that, Brynna."

"Yeah, I do."

"If you walk out that door, you won't be welcome back," he says, his voice shaking.

"I know." I lean up on my toes, pressing my lips to his cheek. My throat aches, my lips quivering against his scruffy skin. This hurts. God, it hurts more than I thought anything could hurt. Because it wasn't Naz who brought us here. It isn't even war that destroyed everything. It's my own damn father and his stubborn inability to just...let it go. To let *me* go.

"Take care of yourself, Dad," I whisper. "I love you."

He closes his eyes, shutting me out.

I turn, running for the door as tears slip down my cheeks. The sob I've been holding at bay claws its way up my throat, a broken, brutal sound. It's the loss of childhood, of innocence. Of everything familiar.

Naz is waiting for me down the street, as if he knew I'd need him. He steps out of the SUV, his amber eyes locked on my face. He doesn't say a word. He simply opens his arms.

I launch myself at him, hitting him like a comet.

He wraps me up in his arms, pulling me into the safety of his embrace. I bury my face against his chest, inhaling his familiar scent—sandalwood, smoke, and something inherently male. His lips brush my crown, a feather-light caress.

"I'm so sorry, little one," he whispers, his deep voice rumbling through me. "I'm sorry it came to this."

The regret in his tone is unmistakable, as if he genuinely wishes he could have forged a different path for me.

A sob wrenches from my throat, the sound muffled against his chest. And then I'm shattering, breaking apart, falling to pieces in his arms as the reality of what I just did crashes into me.

I walked away from my family, from the only home I've ever known, from *everything* I've every known. For him. Because I love him. Because I couldn't bear to lose him.

He doesn't tell me it'll be okay. He doesn't whisper promises he can't keep. That isn't Naz. He doesn't lie, not to me. He simply gathers up the broken pieces of my heart, holding me together...shielding me with his strength because I have none left.

And then he lifts me into his arms, sliding into the back of the SUV with me, and takes me home. Toward the future we've sacrificed everything to build together.

"Make me forget," I plead as he strips me bare in the privacy of his bedroom—our bedroom—in his mansion in Calabasas an hour later, his hands gentle against my skin. I feel calmer but stretched thin.

I need his hands on my body. I need his claim pressed into my skin. I need to be his, broken open and shattered for him.

His hands tighten on my hips without hesitation as he lowers me to the bed, his touch a searing brand shutting out everything but this—everything but us. He follows me down, his weight grounding me in the moment. In him. In us.

"*Mi alma.*" His lips find my neck, trailing scorching kisses everywhere he can reach. "*Mi luz.*" He nips my pulse point, sending an addictive kind of pleasurable pain skittering through my veins. "*Mi vita.*"

He paints a trail of devotion across my body with his lips, with his hands, with every word he breathes into my skin. His teeth close around one of my nipples, and my back bows off the bed, the shards of ice around my heart melting.

His fingertips dance across my abdomen, tracing every imperfection as if he intends to memorize them—as if he already has. I gasp and quiver beneath him, delirious with pleasure, with the sight and feel of him.

He's soft with me, gentle in a way that's foreign and beautiful and so damn devastating. It's like he's determined to put me back together again with nothing more than the strength of his devotion, the fervor of his worship. And damn him, it's working.

I wanted to break. To crumble and burn. He won't let me. He builds me up instead, breathing iron and fire into my veins, into my soul.

"Naz," I whisper his name like a prayer as he settles between my thighs, spreading me wide.

His molten gaze locks with mine as he dips his head, inky black strands of his hair falling over his forehead. His tongue flicks out, the tip of it settling against my clit.

My back bows off the bed, a broken moan tumbling from my lips. This isn't fucking. It's rapture. Divinity.

"That's it, *mi amor*," he murmurs, his breath hot against my pussy. "Let me hear you."

I'm the one who was just tried and convicted, sentenced for loving him, but he eats me like a condemned man savoring his last meal, one seeking absolution between my legs.

His lips close around my clit, flicking, laving...reducing me to a sobbing, shuddering mess of ecstasy. The pleasure crests higher, higher, higher. Until it rips me open and shatters me apart.

I fall with his name on my lips, writhing in sweet torment as waves of his devotion crash through me, unmaking me all the way down to my bones.

He works me through it, bringing me back down with crooning praise and the gentle flick of his tongue against my clit.

Tears spill down my cheeks as he kisses his way back up my body, his lips settling against mine. I taste myself on him as his weight blankets me, as he claims my mouth in a kiss so full of possession, of devotion, I forget to breathe, forget my name. I forget everything that came before him and this moment.

The past doesn't hurt when the present is so good I can't even feel it.

"Are you ready for more, little one?" he rasps against my lips, notching his cock at my entrance. His body is tense and rigid above mine, trembling with need. But he doesn't move, doesn't take what he wants. He waits for me to give him permission.

I rock my hips in silent invitation, in a plea. "Please, Naz. More."

His gaze tangles with mine, never deviating as he presses forward, each thrust slow, deliberate...until his hips are flush against mine, and we're both drowning in ecstasy. We groan at the same time. Tremble in unison.

I'm so full of him, so consumed by him, there isn't a single place in me that doesn't bear his brand. That doesn't belong to him.

He presses his forehead to mine, rocking into me just as slowly, just as carefully as he entered me. He ruins me in a way he never has, breaks and unmakes me with each thrust, each touch. And then he puts me back together again with his forehead against mine, his voice rough with emotion. "*Te amo*, little one. I'll love you forever."

"I love you." Tears spill down my cheeks as I clutch him to me, trying to merge us into one being—not Naz and Brynna, predator and pawn, not the god of war and an Irish *princesa*, but us, this, one soul permanently joined.

"Then marry me, Brynna. Be my queen."

My gaze flies to his, a startled gasp on my lips. His words so closely mirror my own thoughts, my own desires, for a minute, I think perhaps I've only imagined them. But the way he looks at me, the savage beauty painted across his face as he patiently waits for my answer...he said it. He meant it.

"W-what?" I ask anyway, needing to hear it again.

"Marry me." He brushes his nose against mine. "Be my wife, my queen. The center of my fucking world."

My answer tumbles from my lips without hesitation, without thought. "Yes, Naz. Yes."

Possession flares in his eyes, running so deep it steals my breath. His lips crash against mine, his kiss searing, branding. His control slips as he rocks into me, every thrust deep, devastating.

I wrap my legs around his waist, tilting my hips to take him deeper. Harder. I want to feel every inch of him, want him imprinted on my soul.

"That's it, *mi amor*," he groans, lacing our fingers together over my head, his hips snapping against mine. "Fuck me back. Take everything you need from me."

I cry out, digging my heels into his lower back as he grinds against that sensitive spot inside me. Pleasure spirals through me, coiling tighter and tighter. But I need more. I need everything he has.

"Naz," I whimper, clawing down his back. "Please..."

"I know, little one. I know." He slides a hand between our bodies, his fingers clamping around my throat. He squeezes firmly, pinning me beneath him, cutting off my air supply...pushing me closer to the edge. "Let go, Brynna. Let me feel you fall apart on my cock while you're gasping for breath, frantic for it."

His hips snap into me with punishing force, driving his cock deep as his fingers tighten around my throat.

Dark spots dance across my field of vision as my lungs scream for oxygen. The burn is exquisite, the loss of control intoxicating. I'm utterly at his mercy, my body his playground.

"So beautiful," he growls, his amber eyes feral with desire. "Surrendering to me, gasping for me, choking on your need for me."

His words wreck me, splintering me apart. I shatter, convulsing around him. He rips his hand away from my throat, allowing me to pull in a breath...and that sends me rocketing even higher, sends me streaking across the freaking sky like a comet.

Wave after wave of pleasure rolls through me, stealing my breath, my sight, my sense of self. There's only him, only this, only us.

"Fuck, Brynna." His hips jerk once, twice, and then he's coming with a shout. Filling me with his seed, with his claim.

We stay locked together as we come down, both trembling, both gasping for breath. He rains kisses across my face, pouring his devotion, his adoration, down upon me.

"I love you so much, Naz," I breathe, cupping his face in my hands. "So damn much."

"I love you too, *mi alma*." He brushes his nose against mine, pulling me into his arms. "Always."

I close my eyes, listening to the wild thrum of his heartbeat beneath my ear. Reveling in the way he holds me so tightly, as if I'm something priceless, something he cherishes.

Tears prick my eyes, my bottom lip quivering. This is worth any price. He is. I'm not wrong about that. About him. I just wish my father could see it too, could see the way he loves me.

"He loves you, *mi amor*," Naz whispers as if reading my mind. He strokes his down my back, comforting, soothing. "He loves you."

"I know." I swallow hard, my throat burning. "But that doesn't mean he'll ever forgive me for choosing you."

"He will." He tips my head back, forcing me to look at him. His amber gaze is somber, glinting with determination. "I'll find a way to fix this for you, Brynna. Whatever it takes, little one. I promised you that you wouldn't be hurt. I intend to keep that promise."

I'm not sure how he intends to do that, but I hear the conviction in his voice, the absolute determination to keep his promise to me. I see it reflecting in his eyes.

And I let myself hope.

CHAPTER THIRTEEN

Naz

"Let me get this straight," I say, my eyes narrowed at Brynna. "I tell you that we can go anywhere, and this is where you choose?"

"Yes."

I stare at her for a long moment, fighting to urge to tell her I changed my mind. In the three days she's been with me, she hasn't asked for much. She's been quiet, withdrawn. The only time she comes alive is when I'm inside her, fucking my way into her soul, claiming it. The rest of the time, she's lost in her own mind, her own worries. I thought getting her out would get her mind off things.

I may have to draw a goddamn line in the sand here, though.

I flick my gaze out the window again, sizing up the line of people waiting outside. Most have their heads down, staring blearily at the ground, lost in their own worries, in their own fears and anxieties. None of them look like much of a threat, but...

"What the fuck are we doing here, little one?" I ask, genuinely mystified why she chose a soup kitchen of all places.

She glances over at me, quiet for a long moment, and then she sighs. "Do you know why my dad gives so much money away, Naz?"

"To hide the shit he does."

She shakes her head, smoothing a wrinkle in her skirt. "No," she whispers. "It's because, despite all his flaws, despite everything, he's Irish. And one thing we understand is what it's like to go without, to be forgotten, to go hungry, to have nothing. He doesn't give because he wants to hide who he is. He gives because, despite what he does, giving is part of who he is. It's in his blood." She shrugs, one shoulder bouncing. "I guess it's in mine too."

Well, fuck.

I kill the engine, resigning myself to the fact that I'm going to be spending the afternoon slinging soup. The god of war...doing fucking charity. Nicolas would lose his mind if he knew. But fuck it.

Better this than another afternoon questioning my own people. I've spent the last two days doing that bullshit, pouring through every name, looking through every piece of information. So far, we've found at least three with ties to Rojas. Three. And who knows how many more we'll find before we're done before we're done.

But I'm not sure any of the three I've ripped apart was the one doling out my fucking secrets to Sullivan. They're enforcers, drug-runners. No one with enough information to make the kind of mess this prick is making of my empire.

"We can do something else," Brynna says softly. "I just thought maybe we could use a little time away from our own problems for once." Her shoulder bounces in a shrug. "And maybe a little good fortune."

My lips tip up at the corner as I reach across the console, stroking her cheek. "You believe in karma, *mi alma*?"

"What we do always comes back to us one way or another, Naz."

Fuck. Part of me really wishes I'd killed her father a year ago, the first time he snatched a company out from underneath me. She wouldn't feel the way she does now if I had. That guilty goddamn look wouldn't be stamped all over her perfect face.

Dio. What am I thinking? She'd be down two parents instead of one. And as someone who knows what the fuck that's like, as someone who knows exactly how it feels to lose a parent to violence and bloodshed and this world...I don't want it for her. Not even if the prick does deserve it for breaking her heart.

"Come on," I murmur. "Let's go feed your homeless."

"They aren't my homeless, Nazario. They're the city's homeless," she says primly. "And you should care about that too, you know. You may be a criminal, but that doesn't mean you can't be human, too."

A smile twists at my lips, my cock stiffening at the way she calls me out without hesitation, without compunction. Fully grown men wouldn't even dare, but this little *princesa*? She fears nothing, least of all me. I fucking love it.

"Out of the SUV, *princesa*. Before I decide to show you just how big of a degenerate criminal I am in front of all these people," I growl, smirking at her. "Think they'll try to stop the big bad cartel boss if he stuffs his cock down your throat on the sidewalk?"

"Probably." Her pulse thrums against her pretty little throat, her eyes darkening. "But I won't."

Jesus fucking...

The shrill ring of my phone rips through the SUV, freezing me as I reach for her, intending to drag her into my arms.

"Motherfucker," I growl, snatching it out of the console. My mood plummets when I see Nicolas's name on the display. "I need to take this."

Brynna nods.

"What?" I snap as soon as I have the phone at my ear.

"*¡Se nos creció el enano*!" he growls. The dwarf has grown on us—our problems have gotten bigger. Fucking great.

"What the fuck happened?"

"We're on the verge of losing another shipment, *príncipe*."

Anger slices through me, sharpening to rage. "How the fuck are we going to lose another one, Nicolas?"

"Our ship was quarantined as soon as it docked in Aruba, Naz."

"Motherfucker," I swear, slamming my head back against the seat. This is the last thing I need right now.

"They're going to want to hear from you directly, *príncipe*," Nicolas says. "They won't negotiate with anyone but you."

I flick my gaze in Brynna's direction, guilt sliding through me. She needs a day away from this shit. But if we don't get this sorted out before they board the motherfucking ship, they'll rip it apart and take everything. And docking another ship in Aruba will cost two or three times what it does now to keep them looking the other way. We need that port.

"I'll be there," I sigh, a wave of defeat coursing through me. This empire is a yoke around my neck...but it's still my responsibility.

Cristo. Burning it to the ground looks better and better every day.

I disconnect, dropping the phone into the console.

Brynna meets my gaze, hers worried. "What's wrong?"

"Issue with a ship," I mutter, scrubbing a hand down my face. "I have to deal with it, *mi alma*."

"Okay," she says softly. A moment later, her hand slips into mine, her fingers lacing through mine. "It'll be okay, Naz."

I glance over at her, startled. "I'm supposed to be the one telling you that, Brynna."

"Yeah, well, I think maybe you need to hear it sometimes too. You're carrying the whole world on your shoulders. Now, you have help. You have me." She smiles at me, so sweet I want to crawl into her fucking skin and pour myself into her veins. *Cristo*. The way she looks at me, the way she makes me feel... It's terrifying and exhilarating, setting me on fire.

I lean over the console, devouring her lips. I lick into her mouth, claiming every corner of it. And then I pull back, reaching for the door handle. "Stay right here, *mi alma*. I'll be right back."

Her brows furrow with confusion. "Where are you going?"

"To do a little charity and get you that good karma." I wink and then slam the door, striding toward the entrance to the soup kitchen. The fact that she thinks she needs to pour more good into the world to balance the scales for herself is fucking heartbreaking. So is the fact that Sullivan is too goddamn blind to see the damage he did to her.

He put her on a pedestal, turned her into a target, and then killed anyone who took a shot at her. And she's the one who suffered for it. He should have handled it a long time ago.

The moment the first enemy made a move against her, he should have gone scorched earth, burned their fucking worlds to the ground. No one else would have dared try. She wouldn't feel so guilty now if he had. But he let it continue, instead picking them off one by one like it was a game.

I won't make the same mistake. I won't lock her away. She won't be a target. And she'll never know just how brutal and monstrous I'll be to ensure it. Those sins will be mine, carried in secret so they never touch her.

"I need to see whoever the fuck is in charge around here," I mutter to the man standing at the door, letting people in one by one. "I'm about to make his day."

He flicks his gaze up at me, a smile already forming on his lips, and then he realizes who I am. It freezes, half-formed. "Uh..."

"Just go get whoever the fuck I need to write the goddamn check out to," I sigh, not in the mood for this bullshit. "Now."

Shock flares in his eyes. But he's smart enough not to ask a single damn question. He darts inside, running to do as he was told.

"I'm sorry," Nicolas says, scrubbing a hand down his face as we stride back toward my office a full four hours later. "I should have been paying better attention."

He's right. He should have. So why the fuck wasn't he?

I just had to work a miracle and threaten to build my own fucking port in Bonaire because he failed to notice that the payment to our contact in Aruba hadn't been sent. Greased palms pave the way. Dry palms are a motherfucking problem.

I cut my eyes in his direction. "So why weren't you, Nicolas? What was so goddamn important that you forgot what the fuck I pay you to do?" I growl, trying to figure him out, to pin him down.

Suspicion is a cold, hard knot in the pit of my stomach. I don't want to believe it. He's been ruthless over the last few days, cutting through the ranks without mercy, killing without remorse when necessary. And yet...the knot remains.

Where the fuck do his loyalties truly lie?

"You, *príncipe*," he says, dropping his hand from his face to meet my gaze. "You are the reason I forgot."

"Excuse me?" I hiss, my hands clenching into fists.

"I do not mean it like that," he says. "I mean only...you are what was more important, Naz. You have had too much on your plate, too many things pulling at you. We have Sullivan, and the war with Rojas, and the men he's planted here." He shrugs. "It's been a busy time."

I grit my teeth, not buying the excuse. Nicolas isn't careless. And he hasn't seemed all that concerned.

"Your concern is touching, Nicolas," I say, a bite in my tone.

He hears it, a protest forming on his lips.

I throw my hand up, silencing him. I don't want to hear it. Whatever it is, I'm sure it's more bullshit. "I don't pay you for your concern. I pay you to do your job. So do your fucking job or get out."

Nicolas stares at me for a long, silent moment, his dark eyes inscrutable. A muscle ticks in his jaw, his lips pressing into a thin line. "You've changed, Naz," he says finally, his voice soft...disappointed.

"Yeah, I have," I mutter, meeting his gaze. I'm not ashamed of it. I won't apologize for it. If that's what he expects, he's forgotten who the fuck he's dealing with. And perhaps that's precisely the problem. He's forgotten who he's dealing with. "And it's about goddamn time people realized it, Nicolas. This is my organization, my crown, my rules. If I want to burn it to the ground, that's my decision. Don't like it? Not my fucking problem."

He shakes his head, opening his mouth to say something, but whatever it is...I don't care anymore. I've heard everything I need to hear and seen everything I need to see.

Nicolas is my motherfucking rat. He's working for Rojas. And I have to kill the one man in this city I trusted like a brother. But not here, not now. I need one night to process this shit first because this one? This one fucking hurts.

Cristo. If this is what charity buys, Sullivan can keep it.

"I want this little fuckhole," I growl, pressing my thumb into Brynna's asshole as she writhes on my cock in bed two hours later, sobbing my name.

"Naz," she whimpers, rocking back against me, her cunt clamping down around my cock like a perfect vise.

I crane her head back, tugging hard. "I'm taking it, *mi alma*," I snarl against her throat, pumping my thumb in and out of that perfect hole. "Don't tell me no."

We both know she isn't going to deny me. She was on my cock as soon as we walked through the door, begging for it. And I'm a greedy motherfucker, desperate to stay lost in her. She's peace. The only part of my world that has any light left in it.

I'll purge my darkness in her, bury my sins in her soul. She can take it. She was fucking born to do it.

Her juicy pussy clenches around me again, wet enough that I don't even need lube to spread her little asshole open. But I use it anyway. I won't ever hurt her. Fuck that.

I squirt it down the crack of her ass, watching with satisfaction as she squirms all over my cock, moaning, groaning, my eager little slut. My fucking world.

"Keep fucking me, *princesa*. Work those hips and take my cock while I split you open for me," I order, slapping her ass. The way it bounces and jiggles...*Cristo*, what a sight. So I do it again.

She sobs in ecstasy.

"You like that, little one? Like having my handprints painted across your skin?" I spank her again, harder this time. Her alabaster skin flushes red. So goddamn pretty.

I slip a finger into her asshole with my thumb, working her open. She rocks back against my hand, greedy for it.

"Filthy little *princesa*." I twist and plunge, fucking her with it while I spank her ass red. "You like having my fingers in your asshole? Like having both of these little holes stuffed full of me?"

"Yes!" she shouts. "Yes, Naz."

"Tell me why, Brynna." I add another finger, groaning at the eager way she takes it. Fuck. She was made for me, made to fuck, made for this.

"Because I'm yours," she sobs. "I'm your little slut."

"That's right." I nip her ear, soothing the sting with a swipe of my tongue. "And you're such a good little slut, too. So sweet. So eager. So greedy."

I slam my cock into her, pounding her perfect cunt until she's trembling on the edge. When she's right there—right fucking there—I pull all the way out, leaving her little hole clenching around nothing, begging and desperate.

She wails brokenly.

"You're not coming until I'm buried in your asshole, Brynna." I haul her into the middle of the bed with an arm around her waist, putting her right where I want her. "I want your asshole strangling me when I come."

"Naz, please, please..."

"Keep begging, *mi alma*. You know how much I love it," I whisper, running my cock all up and down her ass crack, letting the lube coat it. "Let me hear you plead for me to claim this little hole."

I line up at her tight little asshole, rubbing the slick head of my cock around and around it, teasing her with it. "Beg for it, *princesa*," I growl. "Beg me to claim this filthy hole and make it mine."

She moans, pushing her hips back, trying to impale herself on my cock. "Please, Naz. Please fuck my ass. I need you inside me, stretching me open."

Goddamn, I love that sweet voice begging me for the most filthy, depraved shit. It's almost psychotic how much I love it. But then again...no one ever accused me of being a virtuous motherfucker, now did they?

"That's it, *mi amor*. Beg for my cock in this virgin hole," I rasp as I push forward, applying pressure. Her greedy hole resists, fighting me. "Relax and make it easy for me, little one. Let me in."

She whimpers, relaxing beneath me. The tight ring of muscle slowly gives way, allowing the head of my cock to slip inside. Fucking hell.

She gasps, tensing at the intrusion. Strangling the head of my cock in her perfect ass.

"Shh, *princesa*. Just like that," I croon as she slowly relaxes beneath me again. "You're doing so well."

She whimpers and pants as I gradually work myself deeper, groaning at the way her tight little ass strangles me. The pressure and heat are perfection.

I slip my hand beneath her, sliding through her drenched cunt to her swollen clit. I grind my thumb against it, keeping her right on the edge...right where I want her.

"Breathe, *mi cielito*," I remind her as I impale her inch by inch. "Take me deep. This perfect ass was made for my cock."

She moans brokenly as I stretch her wide and stuff her full, my gaze fixated on the way her tiny hole swallows me up. *Cristo*, the sight alone has me ready to lose it. But I grit my teeth and fight against it, determined to make this good for her.

"Your needy little hole is squeezing me so tight," I groan as I slip in deeper. "Does it feel good, little one?"

"Yes," she moans, already trying to rock beneath me, so fucking eager. "Oh, God, Naz. It's so fucking good. More, please."

"Such a perfect little ass slut," I praise, bottoming out in her. She's completely full, completely owned. Completely fucking mine. "Already begging for more."

She trembles and pants, her muscles clenching wildly around my cock. I stay perfectly still, grinding my thumb against her clit, letting her get used to the feel of me stretching her open like this.

"Please, please." She thrashes beneath me, clawing at the sheets.

I flex my hips, making my cock throb inside her. "Is this what you want, *mi cielito*?"

She wails my name, pushing against me, trying to force me to move. "Please, Naz," she sobs, wrecked and ruined for me already. "I need...I need..." Her pussy drips, soaking my fingers.

"Tell me," I demand, fighting like hell to hang on. The need to move, to fuck into her is overwhelming. But not yet. Not until she says it.

"Fuck my ass, Naz! Please!" she sobs. "Please!"

I pull out slowly, relishing the drag of her tight muscles around my shaft, and then slam back in, burying myself balls deep. She screams, her head thrashing against the pillow, crimson hair fanning out in a wild tangle.

I do it again and again, banging the headboard against the wall. Brynna wails beneath me, lost to the pleasure. The sight of her spread out beneath me, taking every inch of my cock and wailing for more, is the most erotic thing I've ever seen. I'll never get enough of her like this—wrecked and ruined and completely mine.

"That's it, *princesa*," I growl. "Be a good girl and take my fucking cock like the greedy little slut you are."

Her pussy drenches my fingers, her muscles clamping around my cock every time I call her a slut, every time I praise her. *Cristo.*

Possessive pride surges through me. She's mine, stripped bare and broken open, every fucking inch of her consumed by me, obliterated by me.

And she owns me the exact same way. Killing for her would be easy. I do that shit every day and don't regret it. But for her? I'd die, give up everything. That's how completely I'm hers.

"Come for me, Brynna," I order as I plunge into her perfect ass over and over, the headboard slamming into the wall with every thrust. "Let me feel this greedy hole strangling my cock as you shatter. Milk me dry."

I grind my thumb over her clit a final time before pinching it between my fingers.

She screams, her body tensing as the sensation sends her hurtling over the edge. Ecstasy crashes through her veins, exploding, making her writhe in the sweetest torment.

Her asshole clamps down around my cock like a vise, squeezing me so tight it's almost painful. I roar at the sensation, giving in to it.

My own orgasm rips through me, the intensity stealing my breath. I spill into her in hot spurts, filling her up, marking her from the inside out as mine. Always fucking mine.

She collapses onto the bed beneath me, trembling and gasping. I follow her down, pressing open-mouthed kisses across her shoulders and the back of her neck, worshipping her sweaty skin with my tongue.

She reaches for me, threading her fingers through my hair. "I love you," she whispers, turning her face to meet my gaze. "I love you so damn much, Naz."

"*Mi alma*," I rasp, my voice raw. "*Mi cielito. Mi todo.*" I never want to move, never want this moment to end. I want to stay buried inside her, right fucking here, forever.

CHAPTER FOURTEEN

Brynna

I'm wrapped in Naz's arms, his body half on top of me, when something startles me awake. My eyes pop open, my heart pounding against my ribcage.

"Naz," I whisper, reaching up to shake him awake.

But he turns his head, the whites of his eyes locking with mine. He heard it, too.

"Shh," he murmurs, his voice barely audible as he slowly slides off me. His hand skims my side, squeezing my hip before disappearing over the side of the bed. He doesn't find whatever he's looking for. I know because his body goes rigid.

"Naz, what is it?"

"My fucking gun is missing."

"No, *príncipe*, it's not."

I cry out, cowering against Naz as Nicolas's voice sounds in the dark. The overhead light flicks on, momentarily blinding me.

My heart jolts against my breastbone in a terrifying thud when the haze clears. Nicolas looms in the doorway of the bedroom, a gun in his hands. He isn't alone. Another man looms beside him, terrifyingly huge, leering at me.

"You motherfuckers," Naz growls, rolling out of the bed to confront them, not caring that he's completely naked. He pulls me up with him, positioning his body in front of me as if he intends to use himself as a shield.

I don't think this works that way, though. Not tonight. Not this time. One of them—probably Nicolas—is the man who has been slipping information to my dad. He's been working for the man Naz hates more than anything. And he didn't come here to talk. He didn't take Naz's gun because he has good intentions.

He came to kill us.

"I told you that you had changed, *príncipe*," Nicolas says softly, stepping deeper into the room. "You should have killed me today. You knew then that I wasn't your man, but you let me walk away. You are weak, unworthy of your father's throne."

"So you went to Rojas? You betrayed your own people for that prick because you're mad at me?" Naz snarls. "Fucking pathetic."

"You betrayed your people, Nazario." Nicolas nods at me. "You chose that *zunga* over them."

Naz growls a warning, taking a threatening step toward him. "Watch your fucking mouth."

"You don't give the orders anymore," Nicolas says coolly as he aims the gun directly at Naz's chest.

I can't stop the terrified whimper that crawls up my throat. My whole body trembles as I clutch Naz's arm, my nails digging into his skin. This can't be happening. It has to be a nightmare.

"Tie them up, Juan," Nicolas commands the giant, nodding toward us.

Juan advances on us, lengths of rope in his hands.

Naz shudders in rage, a terrifying growl rumbling up from his chest. "Don't touch her," he snarls. "It'll be the biggest fucking mistake of your life, Nicolas."

Nicolas smirks in response, his lips twisting cruelly as he swings the gun in my direction. "I'm happy to blow her pretty little head off instead, Nazario," he says. "Would that be better? You can watch the back of her skull explode, watch her brains splatter all over your bedroom wall. Is that what you want?"

Bile rises in my throat, and I swallow hard, fighting the urge to vomit.

"Naz," I whimper, hot tears spilling down my cheeks. This is really happening. We're going to die.

Naz reaches for my hand, his fingers brushing mine as he tries to offer me some small comfort. But before I can grasp them, Juan is on top of us, trying to rip me away from Naz.

"Don't fucking touch her," Naz snarls.

Juan ignores him, shoving me to the floor.

Naz snarls like a vicious, wounded animal, launching himself at the bigger man. He collides with him as if hitting a brick wall. Juan doesn't flinch, doesn't move. But Naz doesn't flinch, either. He's full of rage, of fire.

Until Nicolas strides across the room, shoving his gun up against the side of my head.

I whimper, cold fear sliding through my veins.

Naz immediately stops fighting, stops moving. He goes completely still, helpless terror firing in his eyes.

Juan uses the moment to his advantage, driving his fist into Naz's stomach with brutal force.

Naz lands on his knees with a grunt.

"Naz!" Sobs choke me as I watch, helpless, as Juan yanks his arms behind his back, tying his hands together.

Nicolas's taunting laughter echoes around the room, and I want to launch myself at him. Claw that smirk from his face. But he has the gun...and I've got nothing but rage.

"Are you still sure you chose well, Brynna?" he asks, derision dripping from every word. "Your god doesn't look so invincible, groveling on his knees like a beaten dog."

"Fuck you," I hiss. "My father will hunt you down like the traitorous piece of shit you are."

"Your father?" Nicolas smiles. "He's next on our list, *princesa*. By dawn, Los Angeles will belong to Felipe Rojas."

"How long, Nicolas?" Naz asks, weariness in his voice. "How long have you been playing both sides?"

"Both sides?" Nicolas shakes his head. "There were never two sides, Nazario. There was only ever his side. You were just too blind to see it."

"You've been with Rojas all along?"

Nicolas shrugs. "You think this organization is yours because we put a crown on your head, *príncipe*? I tried to warn you that it takes more than fear to lead. Your people aren't loyal to you. They're loyal to your father. They're his people, not yours. The rest belong to me. To Rojas. He splintered you from the inside while you thought you were waging war." Nicolas's lip curls. "Without her, you never would have seen it happening."

"Jesus Christ," Naz mutters. "You're throwing a tantrum because I wised up to your fucking game."

"No, Leyva. I'm ending it before you undo all the work I put in. Tie her up, Juan." Nicolas steps aside, making room for Juan.

As soon as he moves, I jump to my feet. He isn't tying me up. There's no fucking way I'm letting him do that. Either way, Naz and I are probably going to die. But I'm not going to die with either of these bastards on top of me, forcing Naz to watch the sick things they do to me to break him. And Nicolas is precisely that twisted, soulless, evil type. He'll hurt me just to watch Naz break, just so he can feel like he won.

He isn't Naz's friend. He never has been. He's just a psycho with an agenda, and Naz was a piece to move across the board.

I won't let him do it. Not today.

I take off, trying to make it across the room before Juan gets his hands on me. He's a lot faster than he looks, though.

I'm nearly to the bedroom door when he grabs me by the hair, dragging me back against him.

"Let me go!" I scream in pain, in fury, struggling in his arms.

"Shut the fuck up, bitch," he growls, viciously pinching my nipple to subdue me.

I cry out, digging my nails in his arm. Biting. Fighting like hell.

"I'm going to fucking desecrate everything you've ever loved for touching her," Naz says, his tone black.

"*Cristo*, Juan. Get her under control," Nicolas snaps impatiently. "Whatever it takes."

Juan wraps a hand around my throat, cutting off my air supply. I immediately stop fighting, terror curdling in my blood. Unlike with Naz, this isn't pleasure. This isn't rapture. This is hell. Because Naz would never hurt me. This man will kill me. And if I die, so does Naz.

Naz meets my gaze, torment raging in his eyes. "Let her go, and I'll give you whatever you want," he says, the same pain in his voice. It breaks me because I know he means it. His life for mine, that's what he's offering.

I want to scream and rage, but I can't.

I can't even breathe.

Nicolas laughs as if the offer amuses him. "You bargain as if you have something we want, but you still do not understand. There is nothing, *príncipe*. We simply wish you out of our way."

Juan relaxes his hand around my throat, allowing me to pull in a breath. I choke on it, choke on tears. All this time, I was afraid of the wrong thing. I was so damn terrified the war between my father and Naz would get someone I loved killed, but that was never the real threat. It was always here. It was always this man. It was always Rojas.

I think they hoped my father and Naz would destroy each other. A war between them kept Naz occupied. But I changed everything, changed *him*, and they're mad as hell about it.

"Even if you kill me, my father's people will never accept Rojas as their leader," Naz snaps, anger in his voice. "They will never bow to that *malparido*. He can take the cocaine fields, Nicolas, but he will never win their respect or loyalty. They will never work for him."

"Then they'll die too," Nicolas says as if it doesn't matter to him one way or another.

"Kill me, but tell your man to let Brynna go," Naz negotiates, his gaze flickering between me and Nicolas, desperate. "She has nothing to do with this. She is *la inocente.*"

"I'm not leaving you, Naz!" I cry.

"You will," he says, his voice soft. "I told you that you would be safe with me, *mi alma.*"

"Then you lied to her, Leyva," Nicolas says. "She won't leave this room alive, either."

"If you touch a hair on her head, my men will hunt you to the ends of this fucking earth," Naz growls, murder in his voice. I think he knows he won't be here to do it himself. I think...God, I think he knew as soon as he saw Nicolas that he wasn't leaving this room alive.

The realization breaks me. He isn't fighting for his life because it means nothing to him. But mine means everything.

Nicolas laughs again, his gaze drifting down my naked body in a way that makes my stomach heave. "She's a pretty little thing. Maybe I'll give her a couple pumps before we kill her, no?"

Pure murder contorts Naz's features, twisting them with rage as every muscle in his body goes taut.

"Naz!" His name is a sharp cry of terror bursting from my lips as he launches himself at Nicolas, roaring in outrage, in murderous fury.

He crashes into Nicolas like a wall, knocking the gun from his hand.

"Fuck!" Nicolas roars as they crash to the ground. Despite being tied, Naz fights like hell, rolling around with Nicolas, kicking, headbutting him, using every advantage he can find. Nicolas can't buck him off or stop him. He can't even protect himself.

I don't have any sympathy. He taunted Naz one too many times, pushed him too far when he threatened me. For years, my father and brother have killed for less than what Nicolas just did. I hated it every time. This time, I want this man to pay. I want him to suffer. Because the look on Naz's face and the pain in his eyes—that's unforgivable.

"Fuck this," Juan mutters, reaching into his waistband to pull his gun.

I cry out, struggling in his grasp, fighting to keep him occupied—to give Naz time to deal with Nicolas. Maybe it's a losing battle. Maybe we still die at the end of this. But I refuse to make it easy for either one of these assholes. If they want to kill us, they're going to have to work for it.

My father may have put me in a cage, but I'm still his daughter. And I won't die quietly.

"Stop fighting," Juan growls when I claw bloody marks down his arms.

"Go to hell," I snap, kicking backward as hard as I can. My foot connects with the inside of his thigh, making him grunt. I twist in his arms at the same time, ripping his hand off my arm.

The momentum sends me stumbling to my knees at his feet. Out of the corner of my eye, I notice someone standing behind him, a vase in his hands. I don't know if he's one of Naz's men, but he's here. He's a chance at survival.

I don't think. I just react, trying to keep Juan's attention on me. I reach out, grabbing his dick the same way he did my nipple. I squeeze as hard as I can, hoping it hurts like hell. Hoping I rip his balls off.

"You bitch," he grunts.

The man behind him lifts the vase over his head, cracking him over the head with him. Juan grunts, stumbling forward as his eyes roll back in his head.

I scrabble backward on my hands and knees, trying to get out of the way as he pitches forward, falling in a heap.

My heart pounds dangerously as the man tosses the broken pieces of the vase aside and leans down, snatching Juan's gun from the floor. I stare at him, terrified, shaking. Not entirely sure if he's here to help or not. Not even sure where he came from.

He's familiar, though. I've seen him before.

"Naz!" I scream in warning when he aims the gun at him and Nicolas.

Naz looks up and sees him standing over me with the gun in his hands. He roars my name like a wounded animal, the sound sharp, full of helpless rage.

Nicolas whips his head in our direction, his gaze flickering rapidly from the guy with the gun to Juan and then to me.

"Hands in the air, motherfucker," the man says, pointing the gun at Nicolas.

He slowly does as instructed, untangling himself from Naz and lifting his hands skyward. Defeat rolls through his dark eyes.

The man flicks his gaze in my direction, his steely blue-gray eyes settling on me. Recognition slams into me. I do know him. His name is Michael Kincaid. We go to school together. At least, we did. His girlfriend's family was just murdered in a drive-by. It's all anyone talked about for two days in class. He hasn't been back since it happened.

Jesus. What is he doing here? How is he tangled up in this?

Does he work for my father?

"Eyes off my fiancée," Naz growls at him.

"I was going to tell her she can cover up. I'm betting she's not exactly thrilled to be naked in a room of assholes. I'm guessing you're Nazario?" Michael asks him.

Naz narrows his eyes on him, nodding warily. "And who are you?"

"Kincaid," he mutters.

I grab the blanket off the bed, dragging it down over me, nearly sobbing in relief when I'm finally covered, my body no longer on display for everyone in the room.

"Do I know you?" Naz asks.

"Nope."

"Why are you in my house?"

"I've been asking myself the same fucking question since I walked through the door." Michael nods at Nicolas, who still has his hands in the air. "You want to do something about him before his buddy wakes up?"

Naz cocks a brow, frustrated amusement in his gaze. But I see the murderous fury it hides. The broken terror. He'll never show that to this man, this stranger, but he's shrouded in darkness, ready to commit murder, mayhem, and monstrous acts.

"Would love to," he says, twisting to show Michael his hands. "But as you can see, I'm not currently in a position to help you out."

"Brynna," Michael calls softly. "Can you untie Nazario, please?"

I sniffle and then nod, pulling the blanket tightly around me and tucking it in to keep it in place before I push myself to my feet. I stumble toward Naz, every damn atom, every cell, every piece of me straining toward him, desperate for him.

I throw myself to my knees in front of him, biting my cheek to keep from sobbing out loud. He leans forward, pressing his forehead against mine. A broken, shuddering exhale whispers from his lips, his entire body relaxing.

"Naz," I whimper.

"Brynna." He whispers my name like a prayer, sending tears rolling down my cheeks. "Untie me, *mi alma*. Everything will be okay."

It's the first time he's promised me that.

Nicolas shifts beside Naz, his hands twitching.

"I will shoot you," Michael warns him. "You won't be the first person I've killed recently. Won't even be the second. Or the third."

"*Hijueputa*," he mutters, glaring at Michael. But he doesn't move again.

I scurry around to Naz's back to untie him. The bonds are so tight they dig into his wrists.

"Who are you?" he asks Michael while I work, plucking at the knots with trembling fingers.

"Already told you my name is Kincaid."

Naz nods and then falls silent, waiting patiently for me to get him untied.

"I'm guessing you don't want me to call the cops?" Michael asks him as the damn ropes fall from his wrists.

Naz smirks, a vicious, deadly smile, rising gracefully to his feet. If it bothers him that he's naked, he doesn't show it. Then again, I doubt it bothers him. He's arrogant, cocky. Perfect.

I watch in silence as he yanks Nicolas to his feet with a hand around his throat. He doesn't say a word to him. I don't think he has anything left to say to him. All that's left now is pain and retribution. He drives his other fist into his face twice in rapid succession, brutal, vicious, without mercy, and then drops him to the ground like he's a useless piece of trash.

"Gun, please," he says, hand extended toward Michael.

"Nah, I think I'm good holding onto it," Michael says, shaking his head. There's a weariness in his eyes that I recognize a little too well. I think he's seen enough bloodshed, enough pain.

Naz shrugs like it doesn't matter to him if Michael keeps the gun or not and grabs the rope I just freed him from. Nicolas doesn't try to fight as Naz ties him up, yanking the ropes so tight they cut off his circulation. He doesn't make a sound, doesn't even move. He just stares blankly at the floor, like he knows his life is over. He rolled the dice and lost, and he isn't the type to beg. Snakes never do.

"You know Rojas will win this war, *príncipe*," he says only when Naz has him tied up. "He'll send others to finish the job."

"Then let them come," Naz says, his voice lethally soft. "I'll kill every motherfucker he sends my way. Starting with you."

I cry out, startled when Naz backhands him across the face so hard he tumbles sideways. His head cracks against the side of the dresser hard and he goes limp.

Naz watches, vicious satisfaction blazing in his eyes, and then turns to me, holding out his hand. "Come here, *mi cielito*."

I don't move for a moment, though. I can't because I'm not looking at Naz. I'm not looking at Nazario, either. This is the monster—the man his people call *Dios de la Guerra*. This is their God of War. And I've never met him before now.

He's been locked away, caged by the man who loves me. But the one who tried to hurt me just set him free. And he's capable of unspeakable acts.

But even the god of war has a soul. Even the monster knows love. And even in the midst of his rage, he needs me.

"I will never hurt you, Brynna," he murmurs, his voice soft. "My life before yours. You will always be safe with me. Remember my promise, little one?"

Tears spill down my cheeks as I fling myself at him. He catches me against his chest, engulfing me in his arms. His eyes drift closed.

"*She's safe*," he breathes, talking to God, to the universe...to fate. "Thank God she's safe."

Sobs wrack my body as I cling to him, trying to press myself into his skin, to remind us both that we're still standing. That, somehow, we survived this.

"Wait," Naz says, and I lift my head to see Michael inching toward the door.

He stops, glancing back at us.

"Who are you?" Naz asks him again.

"I told you my name is Kincaid," Michael mutters, frustration seething in his tone, as if he doesn't understand why Naz won't just let it go. But he doesn't know this man the way I do. Naz can't let it go.

"Your first name?"

Michael hesitates.

"You saved Brynna," Naz murmurs. "I'd like to know who to thank for that."

"Michael."

"Michael Kincaid." Naz nods as he repeats the name, committing it to memory. "Why are you here, Michael Kincaid? Who do you work for?"

"I don't work for anyone. I'm just trying to get the hell out of this city," Michael sighs. "My bike broke down outside. I came to use your phone to call a tow truck. Your door was open, and she was screaming. Didn't like that much."

Naz eyes him, skepticism written all over his face. But I believe him.

For the first time, perhaps in his life, Naz put a little good into the world today. He did charity. At least, he wrote a check massive enough to ensure the homeless in this city won't go hungry for a long time. I think Michael Kincaid showing up here and now might be his karma—the answer to his prayers. A reminder that even monsters can balance the scales.

But I don't tell Naz that. That's for him to work out on his own. Instead, I tell him what I know for sure.

"He's telling the truth," I whisper in his ear. "I've seen him on campus. We have a literature class together."

His expression morphs from uncertainty to acceptance, his faith in me absolute.

"You're a student. You go to UCLA?" he asks Michael.

Michael grimaces, a wave of pain rolling through his expression. "Not anymore," he rasps.

"Why not?"

Michael clamps his jaws shut, refusing to answer. Or maybe he can't. Some pain is too raw, too awful to speak out loud.

"His girlfriend's family was murdered," I murmur to Naz, speaking it for him. "A rival gang shot them to death on her birthday."

His arms tighten around me as if he understands a little too well what that's like. And I guess maybe he does.

Naz doesn't ask any questions. He just processes and accepts it, leaving Michael privacy to deal with his own messed-up world.

"I'll help you get out of Los Angeles," he says.

Michael's eyes narrow on Naz, suspicion heavy in his gaze. Naz sees it, too, and understands it, too.

"You helped me," he says. "You saved my life and that of my fiancée. I owe you a debt of gratitude. Getting you out of the city won't balance the scales, but it's a start at least, yes?"

Michael hesitates for a long moment and then lowers the gun. "Yeah," he agrees. "It's a start."

CHAPTER FIFTEEN

Naz

"Stay in the car, *mi alma*," I murmur, staring out at the mansion where Brynna grew up as dawn lights the horizon. It's been a busy night. I loaned Michael Kincaid a car and enough money to get him out of the city. I don't know what crimes he's committed, what sins he's running from that put him in our path tonight, but I owe him everything for not walking away. Most would have.

Instead, he saved the only thing in this world that matters. If hiding his crimes and helping him disappear is what he needs, I'll bury them under a fucking mountain and ensure this city forgets he ever existed.

Getting him out was the easy part of the night. Everything that came after? Well, the blood that stains my soul now hurt more than it fucking should. But it hurt

Nicolas more. And it was worth every goddamn scream I wrenched from his broken body.

"Naz," Brynna says softly, my name a protest on her lips.

"Please, little one."

She huffs a breath, grumbling quietly. "Fine. But if you get hit again tonight, it's your only fault."

The ghost of a smile paints my lips as I glance over at her. "You think he'll hit me?"

She shrugs, her expression disgruntled. But I see the anxiety behind the mask, the worry. Even now, she fears for my safety, worries that we've pushed her father too far. And perhaps we did. Perhaps we should have handled shit a different way, gone about *us* all fucking different. Too late. We didn't.

And I know something she doesn't. Sullivan may hate me for taking her...but he loves her infinitely more. And Rojas just declared war on both our houses. On her. Nothing unites motherfuckers like us quite like giving us a mutual enemy to hate, to destroy.

It's time to destroy.

I brush my thumb over her bottom lip, watching the way irritation bleeds from her eyes, replaced with lust. It's good to see, not because we have time to fuck right now—we don't—but because after the trauma of tonight, I wasn't sure what to expect with her. But Brynna is a *princesa* to her fucking core. My *princesa*. She doesn't break. She's soft, malleable, able to endure because she can adapt.

People like me and Sullivan, people like Nicolas, we tend to think you need to be the opposite. That this world takes darkness and granite skin to survive it. People like Brynna know better. They live better. They endure because they adapt. They survive because it's who they are. It didn't have to be beat into them like it did with us. They were born with souls that never flag, with light that can't be tarnished no matter how much bullshit is poured over it.

"He isn't going to hit me, *mi amor*. Trust me."

Those are the magic words, the ones she can't resist. She trusts me the same way I trust her—with every fucking piece of me.

"Okay," she whispers.

I brush my lips across her crown, breathing her in, saying a prayer. That she's mine. That she's here. That Nicolas didn't get his filthy fucking hands on her. I broke every bone in Juan's hands for daring to put his on her. One by motherfucking one.

"As soon as this is done, I'm going to work on putting my kid in you, *mi alma*," I murmur.

She shivers, whimpering quietly. I know she wants it. She wouldn't let me fuck her the way I do if she didn't. Who knows? Maybe planting my kid in her will soften her bastard of a father. Heirs have a way of doing that.

I climb from the SUV, striding toward the front door. It takes five minutes of constant banging before Sullivan practically rips it off the hinges to glower at me, wild-eyed and disheveled.

"You've got a lot of fucking nerve, Leyva," he snarls, hatred painted across his face. "Give me one good reason I shouldn't shoot you right fucking here."

"I'll give you three. Follow me." I don't wait to see if he's following; I just turn on my heel, heading back toward the car.

Five seconds later, he mutters a curse, stomping out after me. His steps falter when he sees Brynna sitting in the passenger seat, but when she meets his gaze, he quickly glances away.

Stubborn fool.

I lead him to the back of the SUV, using my key fob to open the hatch.

He rears back when he sees Nicolas and Juan hog-tied inside, both bloody and battered. Both beaten within an inch of their lives. Neither is conscious now, but they were for most of what I did to them. I made sure of that. Pain is art. Rojas taught me that. Nicolas turned me into a goddamn master.

I made sure he regretted it.

I'm going to have to burn the SUV to get rid of this evidence, but the state he and Juan are in? Every one of their screams was worth the effort. It was worth the pain.

"What the fuck is this, Leyva?" Sullivan growls, his eyes locked on the men in the cargo hold.

"A gift," I murmur. "Torture them further. Kill them. Make them suffer however the fuck you want."

"Why?"

"They put their hands on your daughter."

Sullivan's eyes widen.

I nod at Nicolas. "He's been giving you information about my organization for the last year, and you never stopped to question why. He works for Rojas, Sullivan. Did you really think Rojas would leave you and yours alive when he was done using you in his little game? If you did, you're a fucking idiot."

Sullivan's mouth tightens. "Don't piss me off, Leyva."

"No," I snarl, beyond playing nice. "You don't piss me off, Sullivan. They attacked tonight. They put their fucking hands on her, intended to kill her. And *you could have stopped it*." I glower at him, rage boiling in my veins. "She's the only reason I'm not lining your body up beside theirs. She loves you. She needs you. So you don't piss *me* off, motherfucker. Take your gift and be grateful I'm standing here offering it at all."

"Jesus," Nolan mutters, cracking. His hand shakes as he brushes it down his face, glancing toward the front of the SUV where Brynna sits in the passenger seat. He can't hide the worried lights in his eyes, the guilt or fear. "They attacked her?"

"Yeah, they attacked her." I slam the cargo hold closed, meeting his gaze. "It's the last fucking mistake Rojas will make. You may hate me. I don't care. But right now, I need you to hate him more. If she matters to you even half as much as she matters to me, love her enough to hate him more."

Nolan eyes me for a long moment and then jerks his chin in a nod, his expression softening incrementally, as if, for once, he's seeing what's right in front of him. He realizes that Brynna isn't a game to me. She's something I'll die to protect. "What do you need me to do, Nazario?"

I meet his gaze, mine filled with rage so cold it's turned to ice. "Keep her safe no matter what because every single motherfucker Rojas planted in my organization is going to die."

Nolan stares at me for a long, silent moment, shock and distrust warring in his eyes. He wants to believe me, but he's spent so long looking for the knife in his back that he doesn't even know what the word means anymore. But he does understand love. He had a wife. He has a daughter and a son he loves, even when he fucks it all up. And that's what sways him now. "You're really going to kill your own men for my daughter?"

"They aren't my men. They belong to Rojas." I meet his gaze, letting him read the truth in mine. "And I'll kill anyone I have to kill because tonight is the one and only time anyone will ever paint a target on her back. I'm not you, Sullivan. I won't wait for them to come and pick them off one by one every time they insult or target her. I'm going to bathe this city in blood until every motherfucker in it knows exactly what'll happen if they even look in her direction."

"And Rojas?" Sullivan asks.

I smile coldly, viciously. "Felipe Rojas is already dead. His goddamn body just hasn't realized that it's time to stop flailing yet."

"Good," Sullivan grunts, satisfaction glinting deep in his eyes. "Destroy the motherfucker, Nazario."

"Keep her safe, Sullivan. Don't let anyone near her while I'm gone."

He jerks his chin in a nod, eyeing me sideways. "I'm still not on board with this."

"And I still don't care," I mutter. "Neither does she. She loves you, but her place is at my side. You won't stop her. You won't stop me, either. So you can either get used to the idea and keep your daughter in your life, or you can cut off your own goddamn nose to spite your face. The decision is yours. But you and I are done with this bullshit. This is the last time she'll be in the middle between us. It's the last time our bullshit puts her at risk. Take it or leave it."

I don't wait for him to respond, instead striding around to the passenger side to wrench open the door. I kneel beside the car, at her feet where I belong. She reaches out for me immediately, placing her hand against my cheek. Her bottom lip quivers.

"I have to go, little one," I murmur, turning my face into her palm. "I love you."

"Please be careful," she pleads, those emerald eyes eating me alive, as if she's afraid this is the last time she'll see me. But that isn't going to happen, not today or any other day. This pretty little *princesa* is mine. Nothing is taking her from me—not her father, not Rojas, and certainly not death.

I'm the motherfucking *Dios de la Guerra,* the god of war. And right now, one final time, I'm invincible.

It takes three days to purge my organization of the stain Rojas placed upon it. I spill more blood than I can clean off, kill more than I can count. It doesn't cool my rage any.

Nothing does that until I slip through Felipe Rojas's bedroom window outside Barranquilla on day five, exhausted, covered in blood...and as calm as the goddamn eye of the storm.

I settle into an armchair in the corner to wait, a bloody bag on my lap. Patient. Cold.

He stumbles in nearly an hour after I begin my vigil, an old fucking man with a lifetime of brutality beneath his belt. He's changed since I last saw him. He's pushing seventy, his hair gray, his face lined. His hazel eyes are still the same—still cold, devoid of emotion.

He doesn't see me at first, too confident that he's untouchable in his own kingdom, that no one would dare come for him here. Most wouldn't. They're too terrified to even consider it. This man has no soul. He's a goddamn demon, hungry only for pain and misery. Seeking only to be worshipped, to rule.

But he created a monster a little bit too much like him in me. This fucking war between us twisted my soul, shaping me in his image instead of the image of my own father. I've got a little bit of demon in me, too. He put it there.

He freezes when he finally sees me sitting there like I own the goddamn place.

"*Qué putas*?" he growls.

"What? Did you think I wouldn't come for you when I was finished killing all your people, Rojas?" I ask, arching a brow, my expression cold. "You aren't that stupid, are you?"

His hand slides toward the gun at his waistband. Even here, he stays strapped. Even here, he trusts no one.

I point mine at him.

"Don't even try it, motherfucker," I growl. "I'll paint the goddamn walls with your brains before you can touch it."

"You will never get out of here alive, Leyva."

"Then we'll die together, Rojas."

He eyes me critically, assessing, calculating, trying to find a way out of this, one where he manipulates me, I'm sure. But that isn't happening. There is no way out for him this time. I should have done this shit a long time ago, but he's always seemed untouchable, the goddamn boogeyman I had to fight. Not anymore. I don't care if it throws the entire fucking region into chaos or upends the drug market and my own empire. He dies tonight.

"What's in the bag, Leyva?" He nods at it.

I scoop it from my lap, tossing it across the room toward him. It lands at his feet, blood splattering the pretty white carpet.

Rojas glances at it warily.

"You like to collect things from your victims, no? I've heard that about you, Rojas. A finger. An entire hand. Some fucked-up momento so when their families look at the body, they know who was responsible, and they fear you." I motion at the bag with the gun. "I collected a few for you."

He glances at me, amusement curling his lips. "These are not my victims, Leyva."

"Yeah, they are," I say softly. "All twenty-three men you planted in my organization are your responsibility, you prick. They're dead because of you. Because you can't stand to fucking fail."

"I've failed at nothing."

"The fact that I'm alive says otherwise," I smirk at him, cold and vicious. "You wanted my family gone, wanted the Leyva name to fall. You massacred my entire goddamn family to achieve it. But you never could kill me, Rojas. You were too fucking stupid to accomplish it."

"If I had wanted you dead, you would have died, Leyva," he snaps, his voice hard, angry. "Perhaps you lived because you were more useful alive. Look at what I've done, *malparido*. You were on the throne, and I've still infected your organization, pouring my people into Los Angeles. I've still taken what I wanted, when I wanted. And I used your name to do it. Your father's people wouldn't follow me outright, so I gave them you. And I gave them war. They've marched to my orders and thought they were railing against me all along."

Shit. Maybe he's right. He's kept this entire country at each other's throats, kept the entire damn drug trade in turmoil. We've fought and clawed for as long as I can remember, trying to hold him off. And he's the only one who has come out ahead.

But the game has changed. I have. I'm done dancing on strings just because I've got a fucking crown on my head. I didn't sign up for this life any more than Brynna did. So I'm not doing shit his way or anyone else's. Not anymore. It's my motherfucking way.

The god of war needs to die. And so does the motherfucker who birthed him.

"Maybe so. Maybe you did infect my organization. Maybe you did have us dancing on your strings," I acknowledge, pointing the gun at him again. "But I'm fucking done, Rojas. This war is over. You never should have let your men touch her. That's what kills you in the end. Not your fucking drugs. Not your goddamn empire. A girl." My lip curls in a snarl. "You pathetic piece of shit."

Desperation lights his eyes as he lunges for me, reaching for his gun at the same time. But I've said what I came to say. Seen what I need to see. I stare him in the fucking eyes when I pull the trigger.

I smile when his blood paints the walls.

And when I walk away, I leave the man I was, the fucking demon he created, lying beside him.

I'm hers now. Her monster. Her god. *Hers.*

CHAPTER SIXTEEN

Brynna

Waiting for Naz to return to me is a special kind of hell. It burns every minute of the day. Fear and anxiety are my constant companions, sinking their claws in deep and refusing to let go.

No matter how many times my father tells me that he'll be fine, I can't catch my breath. No matter how often Niall tries to make me laugh, I can't see beyond the overwhelming emptiness.

For once, neither tries to hide what's happening from me. They keep me informed, as if they're afraid I might break if they don't. It's a small silver lining in a starless night.

He's killing everyone, their god of war set loose on the battlefield like a demon. I don't feel sorry for them. For the first time in my life, I don't feel guilt or regret. I just feel...relief. Rage.

And that's the freedom he gave me. He snatched me out of my cage and taught me that I'm allowed to embrace the dark. I'm allowed to roll in it. It doesn't change who I am. It's just one part of me. And that part is no less worthy than the darkest, deepest, bleakest pieces of his soul. We are who we are, predator and pawn, monster and *princesa*. Naz and Brynna.

On day six, he finally returns to me. I finally breathe again.

The moment he steps through the front door with my father at his side...I crack. And break.

Painful sobs wrack my body as I stare at him. He's battered and bruised but not broken. Never broken. Naz will never be that. He's too big to kill, too fierce to defeat. Too mine to ever be brought to his knees by anyone or anything else. This man bows only to me. Only for me.

"Brynna," he whispers, his amber eyes locked on my face as he closes the distance between us, moving as if pulled by a magnet...the same way we're always drawn together.

He kneels at my feet, pulling me down into his arms. I wrap myself around him, clinging. Crying. Pressing my devotion into his skin with trembling lips and shaking hands.

"It's over, *mi amor*," he breathes, his own hands shaking against my body as he holds me together, shielding me the same way he always does—with his whole fucking soul. "I'm here, and you're safe, exactly like I promised."

That's the thing about Naz. He doesn't lie. Not to me. Not ever.

"What happens now?" I whisper hours later, clinging to him as sweat dries on my skin and his heart pounds beneath my ear. We're still at my father's, in my room. It doesn't feel like a cage with Naz buried inside me, his cum dripping down my legs.

I'm not sure where things stand between them, but they're no longer at war. They're in that tentative place between conflict and peace, the one where everything is eggshells, but it'll be okay in the end. I know it will because Naz won't accept anything less. And neither will I.

I'm not sure my father will, either. Not after all of this. Not even he can deny the way Naz loves me now. It's written in blood, his empire picked apart at the seams. But it didn't fall alone. He took Rojas's with him. That's the other thing about Naz. He doesn't lose. No matter what it costs. No matter how long it takes.

"Now?" He flicks his gaze up to me, his expression soft. Warm. Dark enough to send a thrill racing through me. "Now we gather the ashes and build something new, little one."

"What are we building?"

His hand drifts down my stomach, slipping between my legs. Wickedness rolls through his eyes. Desire sets them on fire. "A family, Brynna. And forever."

I throw my head back, moaning my answer. The only one I'll ever give him.

Yes. Yes. A million times, yes.

EPILOGUE

Naz

"Fucking hell," I groan, wrapping Brynna's hair around my fist as I fuck her pretty little face. "You're too good at this, *princesa*. The perfect little whore for me."

She whimpers around me, her hand slipping between her legs as her eyes water, spit running down her chin. She fucks her fingers, the wet sound making my balls throb.

"You love this, don't you?" I can't help but ask, marveling for the thousandth time that this woman is mine—my wife, my world, my everything. *Cristo*. She fucks and sucks like she was born to be my little slut. And then she wrecks me with her sweetness, with her love. She's been doing it for six years.

I'll never get enough. A flame like this doesn't fade or flicker or die. It blazes as hot as the sun, fueling empires. It certainly fuels ours. We rebuilt from the ground up over the last six years, changed everything. I'm still a brutal motherfucker. But I'm *her* brutal motherfucker.

And she's my untouchable queen.

She moans around my cock, nodding frantically.

"Then come all over that little hand while you choke on my cock, Brynna. Show me just how much you love having my dick shoved down your throat," I order, pulling her hair hard enough to make it sting...exactly the way we both like.

She takes it like the greedy little fucking queen she is, her hand a blur between her legs as she tries to get herself there. I fuck into her mouth, forcing my cock past lips stretched wide to accommodate me, and into her throat.

She shatters with a whimper, her throat closing around the head of my cock. I mutter a curse, ripping myself from her mouth as my balls draw up. I paint her pretty face with my cum, leave it dripping from her chin. *Cristo*. She looks good, wearing me all over her. Marked as mine.

"Beautiful," I groan, working out every last drop. "So fucking beautiful, *princesa*."

She smiles, slipping her hand from between her legs to swipe her fingers through my cum. My dick roars back to life as she licks my seed from her fingers, moaning like I'm the best thing she's ever tasted.

"Put it where it belongs, Brynna. Let me see," I growl, watching through slit lids as she immediately obeys, wiping me from her face, and spreads her legs wide.

I squeeze the base of my shaft as she pushes my cum into her dripping little fuckhole like a good little *princesa*. It mixes with her juices, smearing across her hole.

Fuck. That's pretty.

I yank her up into my arms, my lips coming down on hers in a hard kiss. "I think I'll put another baby in you, *mi alma*. My heir needs a sibling."

"Yes," she whimpers against my lips, writhing.

I'm halfway to the bed with her in my arms, ready to give her what she wants when my phone rings.

"Motherfucker," I growl, whipping my head around to glare at it.

Brynna giggles in my arms. "You should get that."

"And you should sit on my cock, *mi alma*."

"I will after you answer the phone." She tugs on strands of my hair. "Hurry, Naz. Put your baby in me."

Fucking hell.

I storm across the room with her in my arms, snatching the phone up.

"This better be important," I snarl, already lifting her into place, slamming into her. She whimpers, clawing at my arms, at my chest. Fuck, she feels incredible.

"Hey, Nazario."

Hearing his voice is like having the goddamn past reach down the line. I freeze mid-thrust, my eyes locked on Brynna.

"Kincaid," I say.

Brynna's eyes widen in shock. We've kept tabs on him over the years. It's the prudent thing to do when you owe someone a debt of gratitude you'll never be able to repay. But goddamn. I didn't expect the motherfucker to ever call it in. Not after six years. Not after everything he's seen and done in the years since.

I didn't even know he was back in town. When I last checked in, he was still working for the DEA in Seattle, singlehandedly keeping his boot on the necks of their gangs.

"Bet I'm the last motherfucker you expected to hear from today," Kincaid says, chuckling ruefully. "Sorry to burst your bubble and shit, but..."

"You need a favor," I say for him.

"Yep. Wouldn't ask if it weren't important. No offense to you, but asking a goddamn cartel kingpin for help wasn't on my bingo card."

"What do you need?" I ask, slowly rocking Brynna against me. What? Her cunt feels like heaven, and I need a taste of it if I'm going to have to deal with this bullshit. Because I can guarantee that whatever he needs my help with is going to be bullshit. LA has been on the brink of a gang war for months now. But I keep my nose out of their business. They keep theirs out of mine. I have a feeling that's about to change.

"Can we meet? I'll explain," he says. "You aren't going to like it."

"Oh, I'm aware," I say dryly, but I don't tell him no. He saved Brynna's life. I'll owe him for the rest of mine. Whatever he wants won't balance the scales. It won't even come close. But it's something. "Name the place. I'll be there."

"I'll come to you. Be there in an hour." Kincaid hangs up on me.

I mutter a curse, tossing the phone onto the dresser as I push Brynna up against it, yanking her down on my cock. She throws her head back, moaning as I drive into her, pounding my frustration out into her perfect little hole.

I slam into her, one hand fisted in her hair, the other gripping her hip hard enough to leave bruises. I want to mark her, claim her, make sure she knows that no matter what bullshit is about to rain down on us, she's mine.

"You feel that, *princesa*?" I growl against her throat before nipping at her pulse point. "Feel how deep I am inside this sweet little cunt? How I'm splitting you open on my fucking cock?"

"Yes!" she cries, nails digging into my shoulders as she clings to me. "Fuck, Naz, yes! I feel you everywhere."

I slide my hand from her hip to her ass, squeezing one round cheek before landing a sharp smack. She jolts and tightens around me deliciously.

"Remember it, *princesa*," I breathe. "Because whatever the fuck he wants doesn't change that this perfect little cunt is mine. And it doesn't change my plans for it. I'm planting my kid in you right here and now. So fucking come and make it easy for me."

She shatters around me, screaming my name as her cunt clamps down on my cock, milking me for all I'm worth. Her nails sink into my shoulders, pricks of delicious pain that add to the pleasure consuming me.

I thrust into her one last time, burying myself to the hilt as I explode. I pump her full, painting her womb with thick ropes of cum. Marking her inside and out.

She whimpers and shudders in my arms when I grind against her, prolonging the pleasure for as long as possible.

"That's it, *mi alma*," I murmur against her throat. "Take every last drop."

She does, of course. She always does.

I press a kiss to her throat, breathing her in. *Cristo*. The things she does to me. The way I love her. The sex between us is molten, filthy, and depraved, but it doesn't even compare to what I'd do for her, the acts I'd commit to keep her safe. She and our son are my world.

And I owe both to Michael Kincaid.

Fuck.

"What did he want, Naz?" Brynna asks softly, her head against my shoulder.

"A favor," I say.

"What kind?" she asks, pulling back to look at me.

"The kind that requires a fucking criminal, evidently."

She narrows her eyes at me. But I didn't say anything that wasn't true. We both know it.

"Will you help him?" she asks.

It's a good question. I owe him everything. But whatever he wants could put her in danger. I've spent six years ensuring she was safe, that no one even considered coming for her. And they haven't. After Rojas, no one would fucking dare.

But the people Kincaid deals with? They don't give a fuck about the rules. They don't fear anything. Not even a motherfucker like me. Our worlds exist in a parallel, one I carefully ensure never runs up against the other. Other cartels may use gangs to carry out their business. I don't. I have Brynna to protect. And their rules aren't mine.

"We owe him," Brynna whispers, stroking my cheek. "He saved our lives."

"Fuck," I groan, scowling at her as she unravels every one of my fucking reservations with that sweet voice. She's right. He saved her life. He saved my entire world. Whatever he wants...I owe him.

Guess their rules will be mine, afterall. Set by me and a DEA agent.

Jesus Christ. The things I do for this woman.

Brynna smiles softly. "Don't look at me like that, my love. You know it's true." She brushes her thumb over my bottom lip. "Beside, you need a new challenge anyway. Too much peace makes you cranky."

"Peace?" I chuckle, amusement breaking through the frustration in a way only she manages. "*Mi amor, reina de la guerra*, I haven't known a single day of peace since I met you."

She arches a brow. "Do you regret it?"

"Not a fucking chance," I growl, claiming her mouth in a hot kiss. "Not for a single second, little one."

"That's what I thought," she breathes against my lips, clenching and gushing around my cock.

I press her up against the dresser again, showing her exactly how little I regret it. Not even a little bit. Not at fucking all.

AUTHOR'S NOTE

Thanks so much for reading!

Michael Kincaid's story, Fight for You, is now available.

Want more deliciously dark villains? Knights of Fortune (the Devlin brothers), King of Lies (Niall Sullivan), and Prince of Thieves (Adrian) will be available in 2025/2026!

FIGHT FOR YOU

She's an angel. I'm the devil on her shoulder. And this is my swan song. When it's over, I'll either be the monster at the end of this book...or I'll be the man she deserves.

Michael "Cade" Kincaid

Thirty-two. That's how many bullets it took to destroy my world. I know because I counted.

I lost everything that day—including the only girl I've ever loved. January James will never forgive me for destroying her family. I'll never forgive myself, either. But no matter how hard she fights, nothing changes the fact that she belongs to me, body and soul.

She thinks she hates me, but that was before an enemy from the past painted a target on her back. Now, I'm the only man who can keep her safe. I'll burn his world to the ground before I let him touch her.

But when the smoke clears, and she sees just how dark my secrets really are, I may lose her for good.

God help this city if I do.

Fight for You is a dark romance that can be read as a standalone. Please see the TWs on the author's website prior to reading.

NOW AVAILABLE.

FOLLOW NICHOLE

Like free books? Me too! Sign-up for my mailing list at http://authornicholerose.com/newsletter to stay up-to-date on all new releases and for exclusive giveaways and freebies!

Want to connect with me and other readers? Join Nichole Rose's Book Beauties on Facebook!

Grab signed copies of books, book boxes, and more at http://nicholerose.shop.

facebook.com/AuthorNicholeRose/

instagram.com/AuthorNicholeRose

twitter.com/AuthNicholeRose

bookbub.com/authors/nichole-rose

tiktok.com/@authornicholerose

NICHOLE'S BOOK BEAUTIES

Want to connect with Nichole and other readers? We're building a girl gang! Join Nichole Rose's Book Beauties on Facebook for fun, games, and behind-the-scenes exclusives!

ALSO BY NICHOLE

Find links to my books, audiobooks, the suggested reading order, and a downloadable map of how books connect on my website at http://authornicholerose.com!

Her Alpha Series

Her Alpha Daddy Next Door

Her Alpha Boss Undercover

Her Alpha's Secret Baby

Her Alpha Protector

Her Date with an Alpha

Her Alpha: The Complete Series

Her Bride Series

His Future Bride

His Stolen Bride

His Secret Bride

His Curvy Bride

His Captive Bride

His Blushing Bride

His Bride: The Complete Series

Nashville Lights

Black Velvet

His Secret Obsession

A Hero for Her

Claimed Series

Possessing Liberty

Teaching Rowan

Claiming Caroline

Kissing Kennedy

Claimed: The Complete Series

Love on the Clock Series

Adore You

Hold You

Keep You

Protect You

Love on the Clock: The Complete Series

The Billionaires' Club

The Billionaire's Big Bold Weakness

The Billionaire's Big Bold Wish

The Billionaire's Big Bold Woman

The Billionaire's Big Bold Wonder

The Billionaires' Club: The Complete Series

Playing for Keeps

Cutie Pie

Ice Breaker

Ice Prince

Ice Giant

Cold as Ice

Ice Storm

Playing for Keeps: The Complete Series

Full-Length Titles

Crash into You

Mister Gregory

Fight for You

Kill for You (coming soon)

God of War

The Second Generation

A Blushing Bride for Christmas

Piped Down

Love Bites

Come Undone

Dripping Pearls

Echoes of Forever

His Christmas Miracle

Taken by the Hitman

Wicked Saint

The Ruined Trilogy

Physical Science

Wrecked

Wanton

Wicked

Ruined: The Complete Series

Illicit Love Series

Irresistible

Irrevocable

Irreplaceable

Irredeemable

The Galentines Collection

Romancing the Cowboy

Beach House Beauty

Pretty Little Mess

Hitched to the Heartthrob

Club Dionysus

Dear Mr. Dad Bod

Seduced by Sin (coming soon)

Sinful Obsession (coming soon)

Standalone Titles

A Touch of Summer

Dirty Boy

Dirty Little Christmas

Naughty Little Elf

Tempted by December

Chasing Christmas

Dear Santa

Santa Baby

Easy on Me

Easy Ride

Easy Surrender

One Night with You

Falling Hard

Model Behavior

Learning Curve

Angel Kisses

Carmichael Security Series

Truly Mine

Madly Yours

Deeply Hers

Silver Spoon MC

The Surgeon
The Heir
The Lawyer
The Prodigy
The Bodyguard
Silver Spoon MC Collection: Nichole's Crew

Silver Spoon Falls

Xavier's Kitten
Callum's Hope
Snow's Prince
Aurora's Knight

Silver Spoon Falcons

Leia's Playmaker
Aspen's Defense
Gabbi's Goalie

Silver Spoon After Dark

Bound by Bronx
Coming for Coby
Daddy for Davina

Silver Spoon Heroes
Saving His Sunshine
Commanding the Curvy Girl

Silver Spoon Connections

Devil's Deceit

writing with Loni Ree as Loni Nichole

Dillon's Heart

Razor's Flame

Ryker's Reward

Zane's Rebel

Oral Arguments

Grizz's Passion

Garrett's Obsession

The Daddy Claus

Submitting to Slade

Dating the Billionaire

Dating the Grump

Dating the Boss

Dating Her Brother's Best Friend

Paranormal & Fantasy Titles

A Bride for the Beast (writing with Fern Fraser)

Beauty in Darkness (formerly Beauty's Twisted Tyrant)

Valkyrie Bound

Valkyrie Heart

Valkyrie Fate

Valkyrie Soul

Valkyrie Blade

ABOUT NICHOLE

Four-time award-winning author Nichole Rose writes deliciously dirty rom-coms, contemporary and small-town romance, featuring relatable curvy women and the devoted alpha men who can't live without them. From obsessed billionaires to over-the-top hockey players to the firefighter next door, no one is safe from the hilarious, sassy women she sets loose on the world. She loves delivering relatable characters, hilarious banter, and enough heat to make you squirm.

Nichole also writes dark romance as Nichole Fallon.

When not writing, Nichole enjoys fine wine, cute shoes, and everything supernatural. She is happily married to the love of her life and is a proud ringleader in the world's most ridiculous chihuahua circus. She and her husband live in central Arkansas.

You can learn more about Nichole and her books at authornicholerose.com.

facebook.com/AuthorNicholeRose/

instagram.com/AuthorNicholeRose

twitter.com/AuthNicholeRose

bookbub.com/authors/nichole-rose

tiktok.com/@authornicholerose

Made in the USA
Columbia, SC
01 July 2025